SANCTUARY STONES

A May Scott Mystery

by

Judy Comer Franklin

This is a work of fiction. All of the characters, organizations, and events portrayed in this novel are either products of the author's imagination or are used fictitiously. The characters and events in this book are fictitious. Any similarity to real persons, living or dead is coincidental and not intended by the author.

Also by Judy Comer Franklin

Cold Passion

THIS IS FOR COOPER, WITH LOVE.

ACKNOWLEDGEMENTS

I would like to thank the following people for their support, professional writing skills, and practical guidance: Catherine Geissler, Patricia Harrington, Jean McCord, Robert S. Napier, and Karla Stover. Special recognition to Sharon Schultz, of TillieInk.com, for her technical expertise.

Thanks to each of these talented people who helped make this novel come to life.

Chapter One

Autumn didn't want to let go of the Wiltshire plain. There had been several days with wind and rain but the leaves, in their colorful splendor, wouldn't release their hold on the tree branches and fall to the ground. The crispness in the air and sunny days belied the calendar, which indicated harsh winter should have arrived. Lazy smoke rose from the cottage chimneys and left a lingering smell in the air of comfort and home.

Roses spilled over the fences. Apples, some on the ground but more on the trees, were alternately used as weapons for children to throw at each other or to eat, with the sweet juice dripping down their chins.

Birds scratched around in the fields that had been turned under by the farmers' tractor blades. By now, the birds would have started their migration south to the warmer climes of Southern Europe. This year, though, the geese and smaller birds waited for their inbred knowledge to tell them when to take flight. Their calendars were surer than the farmers, who shook their heads and wondered what was happening to the weather. It was the primary topic of conversation in the pubs and no one had an answer but everyone had an opinion.

The young girl leaned out of her opened bedroom window and took in deep lungfuls of air. She loved the smell of autumn and was happy that it had lasted much longer this year. Her bottle-blonde hair, the same shade as her mother's, shone in the sunny afternoon. She turned toward the mirror that hung over her small dresser and pinched her cheeks, which were already rosy. Her blue eyes looked back and she smiled in anticipation of her afternoon. After rummaging around her closet, she pulled out a sweater, although she wasn't sure she'd need it for the ride she was about to take.

Now, all she had to do was sneak out of the house, get her bicycle from the shed in back and make sure her mum saw none of it. She looked at the clock and knew it was time to leave.

She tiptoed out of her room and moved as quietly as possible toward the rear of the little stone house. When she opened the backdoor it made the familiar squeak that usually didn't sound so loud.

"Sarah, where are you going at this time of afternoon?" her mum asked as she rounded the corner and saw her sixteen-year-old daughter halfway out the door. "It's almost time to start our tea. Your dad will be home within the hour."

"I need to go to the library and pick up a book for my school project," Sarah answered, hoping her mum believed the lie. She could feel the slow flush that was creeping up her neck onto her face. "I'll be home before dad gets here, I promise," she said, knowing it was another lie.

Her mother looked at her daughter, saw the flush and asked, "Are you going to the stones? How many times have I told you to stay away from there? The Boat of the Dead'll take you away to Avalon if you don't stop it. You aren't going there, are you, Sarah?"

"No, Mum, I told you. I'm going to the library. I'll see you later, in time to help with dad's tea."

Sarah closed the door and ran for the shed and her bike. Her mother always seemed to know exactly where she was going, but Sarah didn't believe that nonsense about the stones. She had always felt safe there, as if she was in the sanctuary of a church. It wasn't scary at all, no matter all the legends that surrounded the stones.

The busy A303 that skirted the village went out to the area, but Sarah knew another way, across the fields and along a path that, for a little while, followed the River Avon. She didn't like lying to her mum, but she just had to meet him. He had crept into her mind and heart and nothing could keep her from him, even the love she had for her mum and dad.

Her bike rattled over the rough path. The sky was a beautiful robin's egg blue and the journey seemed shorter than it was because she enjoyed being outside on such a wonderful early winter day.

When Sarah reached a small rise, she got off her bicycle and stood for a few moments and took in the splendid view that lay before her. The massive stones that formed Stonehenge stood sentinel, as they had for thousands of years.

She hesitated and wondered at the small voice that she seemed to hear, coming from deep inside of her. "Don't go," it pleaded. "Go home to your mum and dad."

Sarah got on her bike and considered turning around and peddling as fast as she could toward home. She took another look toward the stones just as he came out from behind one of the sarsens and waved to her. She waved and smiled but the voice was still within her, telling her not to go, to turn back now, before it was too late.

March 1965

"Mrs. Waters, you've got to help me," Sarah said between sobs as she knocked on the door of the whitewashed limestone cottage at the edge of the village.

"Go away! I don't want anything to do with any of you from around here," the old voice said.

"I'm desperate, Mrs. Waters. You're my only hope." Tears and terror made Sarah difficult to understand.

A gnarled claw of a hand reached outside the door and creaked it open. "All right, child, come in."

Sarah had never been inside this house but she'd spent plenty of time outside it, especially on All Saint's Eve. It was a well-known fact that Mrs. Waters practiced the ancient arts of the goddess.

"I didn't have anywhere else to go. I'm pregnant, Mrs. Waters, and I don't know what to do."

"Marry the boy." A large tabby cat strolled into the room and sat next to the fire, which burned cheerfully in the grate.

Tears ran down Sarah's face and her tragic eyes told the story.

"So, he won't marry you, will he?" Mrs. Waters had heard this tale told a thousand times. She moved toward a large, soft chair and sat down.

"When I told him we were going to have a baby I thought he'd be happy, like I was. I told him I loved him and he said, 'Well, there's nothing I can do about that. And anyway, how do I know it's mine?' Then he walked off and I haven't seen him since."

Mrs. Waters looked at the young girl and heaved herself up from the comfortable chair. She walked over to a cabinet that covered the better part of a wall and opened one of the doors. Inside, bottles and boxes were stored in tidy rows. "Here's what can help you, if that's how you want to solve the problem." She walked over to Sarah and handed her a small bottle with an undecipherable label on it. "Take this every night for a week and by the eighth day, he'll be gone."

"He?" Sarah asked as she looked at the bottle. It glistened in the firelight.

"Your baby boy," Mrs. Waters said as she carefully watched Sarah's expression.

"My mum and dad would kill me if they knew. I'm their perfect daughter. I've always done everything they wanted. I can't tell them. My mum couldn't show her face in the village anymore. Dad would be the worst, though. He'd disown me. I'd never see them again. I don't want to kill my little baby, but I don't have anywhere else to turn." Sarah put her hands over her eyes and rubbed them, as if she could rub the horror away. "How much do I owe you, Mrs. Waters? I have some money with me."

"Naught. Just think hard about what you're about to do, Sarah. Go to the sanctuary stones and listen to what they tell you."

"I don't know where they are. Tell me and I'll go. Where are the sanctuary stones, Mrs. Waters?"

"You know, child. You've always known."

After Sarah had left, Mrs. Waters went to her wall of books and pulled out an especially outsized one located on the end of the shelf about midway between floor and ceiling. A small girl peeked through an open door and watched as her mother started to work her magic. The child knew that when she'd told Sarah to go to the stones that something important was going to happen.

"Would you like to sit with me, Leslie, as I prepare the spell?" Mrs. Waters had her back to her daughter but could hear the rustle as she ever so slightly opened the door to get a better look. Leslie loved her mother, but was also afraid of her. "No, ma'am, I'll go to bed."

Mrs. Waters knew the effect she had on her only child and she laughed to herself. "She's like I was when I watched my Mum do the arts," she mumbled under her breath. "She'll soon be ready to learn everything I know and then some. Leslie is blessed with the powers of the Lady of the Lake."

Mrs. Waters' fondest hope for the girl was that she would be apprenticed to the Old Ones who lived on the Isle of Avalon. There she could learn the lessons still taught to the very few who were deemed good enough. "I almost made it," she said to herself, proud of coming close to the elusive accomplishment.

Leslie didn't go to bed. Instead she watched as her mother began to transform herself. First, she took off the heavy black robe that covered her body, then removed the old brown scarf that bound her hair. When she was finished, she raised her arms, palms upward, and began to chant in a language that sounded almost understandable. Leslie knew some of the words; she understood "baby boy" and "gift to the lord and lady" but the rest was indecipherable. This was Leslie's favorite time, when her mother did her spells. No one knew that her mother was so beautiful. Her white-blonde hair hung almost to her thin waist and her breasts were large and perfectly round, with rosy-tipped nipples. Her long legs were graceful as she danced about the room, weaving back and forth in a way that was spellbinding. Leslie felt herself being pulled into the room in spite of herself.

She opened the door, dropped her nightgown, and joined her mother in the dance steps that somehow she knew. Her voice chanted words that she didn't understand.

Mrs. Waters looked down at her daughter and smiled. She looked like a miniature replica of herself. It wouldn't be long until she would have to explain about covering her beauty from the world.

"Lady Violet, there's someone here to see you. Begging your pardon, Ma'am, but I believe it might be Mrs. Waters from the village." Mrs. Long moved quickly around the sitting room, picking up an item here and there, in preparation for the visitor. "Do you want me to tell her you aren't receiving this morning, m'lady?" she asked.

"No, I'll see her." Lady Violet gazed out of the window and thought that the gray, overcast day exactly fitted her mood. Nothing would ever be right again since she'd heard the news from the gynecologist she'd visited in London. He hadn't given her any hope; in fact, just the opposite. His words were burned into her heart and tears streaked down her face. "Do you think he told me the truth, Mrs. Long?" Her desolate voice choked back sobs and she leaned on the windowsill.

Mrs. Long sighed. "His diagnosis didn't sound positive and he warned you about trying to get pregnant again." This wasn't the usual kind of conversation that Mrs. Long had with her employer but she felt a kinship with the young woman who, like her, was recently married.

"I feel such a failure. Lord Willsdon has to have an heir. What am I to do? I never should have married him anyway. My father said it was the answer to a prayer, but it's not that way at all. He's so old. Here I am young enough to be his granddaughter and now I'm the one who can't have children. I want to die, Mrs. Long, I just want to die." She collapsed into a silk-covered wing chair beside the window.

"There, there, Lady, please calm yourself. Lord Willsdon loves you so much, it's written all over his face every time he looks at you. But you have to listen to the doctor. He said getting pregnant again might kill you and you're too young to die." She wanted to put her arms around Lady Violet but knew that would be stepping even more out of bounds than she already was. "Are you sure you still want to see Mrs. Waters? I could tell her to come back tomorrow. Wouldn't that be better?"

"It doesn't matter. Nothing matters. I'll see her. She probably wants my help with the jumble sale."

"I doubt it. You've not been in the village long enough to know, Mrs. Waters. She's--special. I don't think jumble sales are anything she's dealt with before." Mrs. Long looked at the young woman to see if she understood what she'd told her.

"Tell her to come up. Please serve us tea, Mrs. Long. Thank you."

"Of course." Lady Violet hadn't understood about Mrs. Waters. That was all right because she soon would.

Mrs. Long walked across the spacious sitting room, opened the door and gently closed it behind her. Her footsteps were silent on the thick rugs that covered the long hallway. She held onto the banister as she carefully walked down the curving stairway to the entrance hall. Ancestral portraits covered the wall. The Willsdon family had held this property, which included the village, since the time of Henry VIII. They had prospered and so had the villagers. As she walked across the marble floor of the entrance hall to the library, Mrs. Long considered whether she should have told Lady Violet the truth. "I should have done," she said out loud as she opened the library door.

"No, you didn't have to tell her," Mrs. Waters responded. "I'll let her know in my own good time, if it becomes necessary. How's the baby?" she asked from the soft cushions of the burgundy colored sofa. The library was dark, even though the heavy curtains had been pulled aside earlier in the morning. Mrs. Waters' shining golden hair was the only bright spot in the room.

"You heard my thoughts about Lady Willsdon before I opened the door, didn't you?" Mrs. Long asked. "As for my baby, I felt her move and it was like a butterfly wing fluttering against my insides. Thank you so much for helping me, Mrs. Waters."

"Ah, that's what I do, isn't it? Come, sit next to me and tell me what's going on that you asked me here. I rarely come out like this, as you know."

"It's Lady Violet. I'm afraid it's going to drive her daft because the doctors in London have given her no hope. She can't have any children and she knows it'll be the end of the line for Lord Willsdon because of it. He's got distant relatives in America but that's not the same, is it now?"

"I knew, of course, there were problems, but I wasn't sure if she'd want me to help her. But you're right, it's for the village, not just Lord Willsdon and his line of succession. Let me go up and visit."

She rose gracefully from the deep cushions and followed Mrs. Long as she led the way to the sitting room. When they arrived outside the door, Mrs. Long knocked quietly and then opened it slowly. "Mrs.

Waters is here, my Lady. Shall I bring her in?"

Lady Violet hadn't moved from the chair. Her eyes were still fixed on the gray day outside the many-paned window. Rain had started and it blew against the window, making a slight pinging sound, suggesting that ice crystals were in it. "Yes, please do," she replied, but didn't change positions to greet her guest.

"I'll just go make some tea. That'll cheer you up on a miserable cold day like this," Mrs. Long said as she exited the room.

"I'm Mrs. Waters," the visitor said to Lady Violet, who still hadn't moved.

"Please, have a seat." Lady Violet gestured toward a matching wing chair on the other side of the window.

Mrs. Waters walked over to the chair and sat down. "Mrs. Long felt I might be able to help you."

"No one can do that. I want to die. Can you help me do that? Can you make me die right now?" She covered her face with her small hands and sobbed. "I'm a failure. All I had to do was to have a baby, but I'm incapable of even that. I'm being punished because I married an old man whom I don't love. I know I shouldn't be saying these things but I'm out of my mind and I don't know what to do." She leaned her head toward her knees and groaned in agony. "I want to die," she repeated.

"It's true I won't be able to help you have a child that comes from your body but I can give you a child, a baby boy. He'll be born before the winter solstice."

Lady Violet lifted her head and turned to look at Mrs. Waters. "What did you say?" Though she'd heard every word she wanted them repeated.

Mrs. Waters smiled. "Your son will arrive in time for Boxing Day."

Lady Violet rose from the chair and looked down at her visitor. "Who exactly are you?" Her voice quivered and her face turned a paler shade than it had been.

"I'm an old one, trained in the ancient arts of the goddess. You will enable the fabric of this village to remain intact as it has for hundreds of years. At the same time, your husband's line will be continued and your dowry contract will be met."

There was a series of taps on the door. Mrs. Long walked into the room after opening it to allow a young housemaid to bring in the tea tray. "Please set it on the table by the fireplace, Gretchen. That will be all." Mrs. Long's voice was different when she spoke to the house staff.

"Shall I pour, Lady Violet?" she asked as she took in the scene by the window.

Leslie hid behind her mother's long skirt as they entered the shoe shop. She couldn't remember a time when her mother had gone into the village. The village always came to her, at least that's the way it seemed to the little girl. She knew her mother was powerful and someday she would take her place as head of the village. Even at her young age she understood the succession. In their way, they were part of a royal family. Her ancestors had kept the village safe and prosperous for hundreds of years.

"Leslie, please stand next to me and stop pulling at my clothes," Mrs. Waters asked her daughter. Her mother looked beautiful today, Leslie thought. Sometimes she scared people, on purpose, when she pretended to be old and ugly. But today was one of the good days and her mother looked like any other woman, only more striking.

"Will I look like you when I'm grown?" Leslie asked.

"In some ways. We have the same color hair but you won't be as tall as I am," her mother replied. "I wonder where Lucinda is. She should be in her shop." She rang the bell that was on the counter. "Of course, since you will be going to the Old Ones soon to continue your training, someday soon your powers will be much stronger than mine, Leslie."

There was a loud thump from behind the curtained door. "I'm coming out in a moment, Mrs. Waters," a voice called.

Leslie had met Mrs. Davis on many occasions so knew that she could sometimes be scatterbrained. It was the total opposite of how she looked, though. Mrs. Davis always dressed in a suit, and her hair was pulled tightly away from her face in a neat bun at the back of her neck.

She entered the room carrying a load of shoeboxes. "Let me just put these away and we can go upstairs. In fact, if you want, go on up and I'll be with you in a moment," she suggested.

"We will."

They went through the curtain into the back of the shop and proceeded up the steep stairs. At the landing, there was a short hall, which ended at a door. Mrs. Waters opened the door and they entered a small room. A window along the south wall let in light. Leslie thought it was dreary and cold. "I don't like this place, Mum." She clutched again at her mother's skirt. "Let's go home," she pleaded.

"We have an important errand, so we have to stay. Let me turn on the light and that will make it nicer for us." She walked over to the switch and turned it to the right. Dim light sputtered on and off. "Must be a short in the wiring."

Her mother began to move chairs around the table that was in the center of the room. Leslie helped as much as she could but the chairs were heavy.

The clumping of feet let them know that the others had arrived for the meeting. Mrs. Davis entered first, followed by Mrs. Joan Pritchard, librarian, and Mrs. Long, housekeeper for Lord and Lady Willsdon. Moments later a man and woman that Leslie didn't know came into the room. She looks scared, Leslie thought.

"We're all here, I see," Mrs. Waters said. "Lets take a seat around this table and proceed. Leslie, sit by me. Someday soon you'll take over these meetings and you're old enough now to start learning how to do it." Her mother pulled out the chair to her right and Leslie sat down.

"I'm going to tell you what we need to do in order to keep our village as it is. The current Lady Willsdon is barren and there is nothing physically I can do to help her overcome that. A few nights ago, Sarah Demming, daughter of Mr. and Mrs. Demming, John and Rachel, who are with us this afternoon, came to see me. Sarah is pregnant and the father of the child left her as soon as he found out." Mrs. Waters paused and looked at each person sitting at the table. "I am going to let Sarah come to term and give her baby boy to the Willsdons to raise as their own."

There was a sob from Rachel Demming. John Demming looked straight ahead and didn't move at all. He looks like a statue, Leslie thought. The others seated around the table looked anywhere but at Mrs. Waters or the Demmings.

"This has been done before, as most of you know. It's the best way to keep things as they are and make certain that we have an heir for the coming years." Mrs. Waters looked directly at the Demmings as she continued to speak. "Your grandson will live a charmed life. He will never need for anything because we will take care of him. Your sacrifice is needed in order for us to keep our village moving forward."

Mr. Demming shifted in the chair. "What do you mean, bringing us here like this. I won't allow it. Do you hear me? My daughter is not pregnant, she's a good lass, and I will not let you make her out to be some sort of wicked woman." His hands were clinched on the edge of the table. It looked as though he wanted to hit someone. Mrs. Demming sobbed uncontrollably and covered her face with her hands. "Why would she come to you, the village witch, instead of to us? Tell me that," he demanded.

Mrs. Waters looked at the couple and said, in her gentlest voice. "She knew you wouldn't help, that you would judge her. She's always had to be your 'perfect daughter' and she couldn't disappoint you. So she came to me. It would have made your daughter's life much easier if the both of you and the boy loved her enough to support her through any circumstances."

"I never judged Sarah. You're talking nonsense. Let's get out of here," he said to his wife.

She had taken her hands away from her eyes and turned to face her husband. "What Mrs. Waters says is true, John. We've expected too much from Sarah, put too much of a burden on her shoulders. We wanted her to live her life to make us proud. You and I did this, John. We're responsible as much as the man who got her pregnant. The two of us made it so she couldn't come to us with her problems."

"She's not pregnant, I tell you. Not my Sarah," he said. His head dropped and his voice sounded less strident. "I never meant to hurt my little girl. She's my life." Tears began to roll down his cheeks and his head dropped even lower. "I didn't mean to hurt her."

Mrs. Waters let the scene play out. "I'll need help when it comes time for the baby to be born. I'd like to use the little garden shed right behind the cottage on the estate. Could you prepare it, Mrs. Long?"

"Of course. It will be done by the end of the week."

"Before Boxing Day, our village will have an heir and Sarah will be our heroine."

May 1965

Mrs. Long gathered the cleaning supplies that she would need to take to the little garden shed to get it ready for the birth of the baby. He wasn't due until near the time of the winter solstice but she wanted to at least get going on what was a big project. "Let's see, I've got everything I'll need, at least for this first attempt," she muttered to herself. No one knew she was going to be doing this, except for the group who met at the shoe shop a few days prior. Mrs. Waters had told her that Steven Roberts, Sarah's boyfriend, would be helping her, and she was glad of that. Otherwise, she wasn't sure how she would get the entire project finished in the manner that Mrs. Waters required. She had given explicit directions on what was to be done. "She's wanting to turn the old potting shed into hospital," Mrs. Long groused, when she realized the extent of the cleaning that would be required. Of course, she kept her comments to herself. She had learned long ago that you didn't go against the wishes of Mrs. Waters.

Finishing this chore, she went outside. The weather was perfect and the red roses were blooming in spectacular fashion. She took a few minutes to sniff the ones closest to her, which covered a large section of the fence that she stood beside. Lady Willsdon's favorite flower was the rose, so the estate was covered in every shade and variety. Lord Willsdon had that done when she had received the news that she couldn't bear children. He loved his wife and hated to see her suffering. The roses were his way of trying to make her happy.

Standing behind a copse of trees, the stable was hidden from the back of the main house. A portion of it was used for storing the gardening and cleaning equipment that was used on the estate. A wooden fence circled the horse paddock and a couple of grooms were trying their best to put a saddle on a young thoroughbred. Lord Willsdon enjoyed nothing better than to work with his horses and he, too, was in the midst of it, and finally succeeded in getting an elegant saddle onto the back of the resisting horse.

As she watched, Mrs. Long noticed the figure of a woman walking toward the estate, coming from the direction of the village. Paths crisscrossed through the forest, and had done for hundreds of years. The path led past the back of the estate, at a great distance, but anyone on the path could observe the buildings and horse paddock. There was a small lake at the edge of the path and the figure stopped for a moment. Curious, Mrs. Long watched as the woman began walking around the lake and down the small incline to the estate.

"Why it's Sarah Demming," she said aloud, although no one was close enough to hear her.

Sarah walked toward the paddock and waved to the men working with the horse. They nodded in greeting, busy with the headstrong animal. She walked around the paddock and soon joined Mrs. Long.

"How are you today?" Sarah asked the older woman.

"I'm a wee bit tired, to say the truth. Been busy getting ready to do a good spring cleaning," Mrs. Long answered as she watched Sarah look at the grooms, who were still busy with the horse.

"It was so beautiful I just had to get out of the house. Mum has me cleaning, too. She, all of a sudden, had the idea that we should pack up our belongings and move away. Have you ever heard of anything so daft?" Sarah asked. Her smile was pretty, and the pregnancy wasn't noticeable, unless you knew about it.

"Where in the world would you be moving to?" Mrs. Long asked. "Your family has always lived in the village, as far as I know."

"It's pure silliness. I told Mum she must be going through the change to come up with a plan like that. But there you have it, she's convinced we need to move to Cornwall and be with her sister."

"What does your dad say about it?"

"He doesn't say anything, as usual. Anyway, if Mum says he has to go, he will. You know how bossy she is."

"What will happen to your cottage?"

"Mum had the estate agent in yesterday. He's going to let it to tourists, if you can believe that. I laughed when I heard it. We don't have a cottage anybody would want to let. I told Mum she might as give it to our neighbor, Mr. Phillips, to use for his chickens."

"He lets those birds run all over the place. Almost ran over one on my bicycle when I came into the village last week on my day off," Mrs. Long said. "When are you and your family going to be moving, then?"

"As soon as we can get our clothes packed and out the door. I've never seen her like this. It's like she's possessed or something. I'd better get going, Mrs. Long. Otherwise, my Mum will be after me even more than she is now. If I don't see you again before we leave, all the best to you. Please give Lady Willsdon my fond goodbyes. She was always so kind to my family. I need to be speaking with James Ferguson for a bit, Mrs. Long, so I'll be going now," Sarah said in farewell and walked over to where the men were. She went up to James, a dark-haired man who'd been working for Lord Willsdon for a few months, and said something to him. They talked for a couple of minutes and then Sarah went back the way she had come.

Mrs. Long noted her progress. As soon as she had disappeared into the dark trees, she headed back toward the main house.

"Mrs. Long," a voice called. "Could I be bothering you for a cold drink?"

James Ferguson walked up to her and said, "I'm fair parched after working with that stallion." He ran his hand, which had an enormous ring on the marriage finger, through his dark hair.

"Of course. I'll get you several bottles of ale and you can take them down to the stables. The others would like a drink, too, after all the work you've been doing."

They continued to walk toward the house and he said, "I saw you talking with Sarah."

"Yes, she told me her family is moving to Cornwall. Might I ask what that big ring is you have, James? It's so eye-catching."

He held out his hand proudly, "I got it in Hong Kong when I was in the Navy. It's pure gold," he said.

Mrs. Long looked at, shook her head and said, "It has a skeleton face on it."

He laughed and said, "It's my lucky ring. I wear it all the time."

They'd reached the back of the house and he waited outside while she brought out the cool ale bottles. "Here you go, young man," she said, handing them to him.

"Thank you, Mrs. Long. Ta ta," he said cheerily and walked back toward the paddock.

After he had disappeared into the stables, she went back into the house and made her way to the telephone in the library, where she was assured of privacy.

Dialing the number, she waited impatiently until it was answered. "I have to see you now. There's a big problem," she said into the telephone, not bothering with etiquette. "I'll be there as soon as I can. I'll tell Lady Willsdon I have to get a letter into the post or some such excuse. No, I can't discuss it over the line. I'll be with you shortly." She replaced the receiver and pondered the situation. "Nothing good about this that I can see," she said and left the room to find Lady Willsdon.

Mrs. Long put the telephone receiver back into the cradle and went to open the library door. She cracked it just an inch and peered into the large entry hall, relieved that it was empty. Shutting the door gently behind her, she walked onto the marble entryway. Mrs. Long held the curved wooden rail as she climbed the stairs to the second level. Lady Violet's suite of rooms was located to the right, at the end of the long hall. Making no noise on the heavily carpeted floor, she tapped gently on the bedroom door.

"Come," a voice called.

Mrs. Long opened the door and entered. "Ma'am, I have an unexpected errand in the village. I'd like to leave for about an hour."

Lady Violet, sitting near the tall double windows, motioned for her to enter further into the room. "The roses are lovely today, aren't they?" she asked, looking once more onto the gardens. "I almost think I can smell them." Lady Violet smiled and the beauty of the young woman struck Mrs. Long again. It was rare when she smiled, and it lit up her entire face. Light brown curls tumbled down onto the shoulders of the sheer pink gown that she wore.

"Would you like to go outside, Lady Violet? I could help you before I leave."

"Oh, no, you go ahead. I enjoy being here, above the roses. My husband planted them especially for me, did you know that?" She folded her small hands into her lap. "He did that when I was told I could never bear his children." Her eyes were dark and sad when she looked up at Mrs. Long.

"Yes, ma'am, he loves you so much. I just saw him at the stable, working with the young stallion. Perhaps I could take you out there so you could watch? It would please him if you were with him." Mrs. Long knew she wouldn't leave the room, although she tried daily to get Lady Violet to go outside and enjoy the beauty of the estate.

"Not today. Maybe tomorrow. Do you believe Mrs. Waters has the power to help me get pregnant? She told me I'd have a baby son by Boxing Day. Is that possible, do you think? I haven't told my husband what she said. I couldn't bear his disappointment if it's not true." Her luminous eyes longed to be told she would have a son.

"If Mrs. Waters says you'll have a baby by December, then you will. Begging your pardon, but I'd like to leave now. As soon as I return, I'll bring your tea."

"Of course, you're so kind to me, Mrs. Long. I'll just look at my roses, then I may take a short nap." She turned back to the windows, leaning forward to better view the beautiful flowers.

Mrs. Long quietly closed the door behind her, then hurried down the stairs and out through the kitchen to the back entryway. Her bicycle was parked next to several others, owned by employees like her, who lived away from the estate. She climbed on and pedaled furiously until she reached the tree-lined path that led near the village. Before she got to the High Street, she made a sharp left turn and got off of the bike to push it along the narrow path that would take her deeper into the trees. The air was still and the woods were silent. Her feet crunched along and the bike rattled as she pushed it along the rough ground.

The limestone cottage looked welcoming, with a thatched roof made from reeds and straw. It sat in a lovely open space that allowed the sun in and was not far from the bustle of the village. As she approached, the door was opened and a childish voice called, "She's here, Mother."

Mrs. Long recognized the voice. "Hello, Leslie, it's me come to visit with your Mum."

Leslie ran out onto the path and pushed the bicycle for Mrs. Long. "She's waiting for you inside. Can I ride your bicycle around while you're visiting? I promise I'll be careful."

"Of course, child. Why don't you have one of your own?"

"For my next birthday, when I'm ten, Mother has promised I'll get a bicycle for my present." Leslie climbed onto the seat and shakily rode around the small lawn. "I need to practice," she said, her long blonde hair shining in the sun.

Mrs. Long watched for a moment and then entered the open door. "Hello, Mrs. Waters, I'm here," she called.

"I'm in the kitchen. Please come back."

The cottage seemed smaller than Mrs. Long remembered. But then, most of her days were spent in the elaborate rooms of the estate. Anything would seem tiny in comparison.

"Have a seat, and would you like a cup of tea after your short journey?" Mrs. Waters asked, as she worked at chopping vegetables. "Leslie and I are having a nice soup for our supper. The fresh vegetables are lovely this year, aren't they?"

"Yes to both of your questions. I can never turn down a cuppa."

"Your telephone call sounded urgent. What has happened?" Mrs. Waters stopped chopping and turned toward the younger woman.

Mrs. Long told her the entire episode of Sarah's short visit to the estate. As she talked, Mrs. Waters prepared both of them a cup of tea. "Do you know exactly when the family is planning on moving to Cornwall?" She asked as Mrs. Long wound down from her storytelling.

"I'd say within the next day or two," she replied, stirring sugar into the hot tea.

"Thank you for letting me know. I'll take care of it. Now, how is Lady Violet doing?"

The two women continued to chat but Mrs. Long didn't forget her promise to return to the estate within the hour.

After Mrs. Long left, Mrs. Waters pondered what had to be done. "It's too bad, but there's no way 'round it," she said out loud.

From behind the almost-closed door of her bedroom, Leslie watched her mother. Using an open window she always left unlocked, Leslie had climbed into the room. She kept a small stump beside the cottage and moved it under the window for just such occurrences as this. That way, she could come and go as she pleased. And her mother knew nothing about it. Sarah wasn't that much older than she was, and Leslie wasn't sure what everything meant that she'd heard Mrs. Long tell her mother, but knew it was important. She had "the look." Leslie had learned early not to get too close to her mother when she had that expression on her face.

Mrs. Waters moved toward the telephone and picked up the receiver. "Hallo, please connect me to the grocery. Thank you."

Leslie moved close to the door opening so she wouldn't miss a word her mother said.

"Yes, this is Mrs. Waters. I need to speak to Steven Roberts, please.

I'll hold while you locate him."

In just a few moments, she said, "Steven, come now. It's time. Yes, I know it's earlier than we planned, but something has happened. I'm going to send Leslie to her friend's house for the rest of the afternoon. We'll be alone."

As soon as Mrs. Waters finished the conversation and hung up the phone, she moved toward Leslie's bedroom and opened the door. The room was empty and she smiled. Walking over to the window, she caught the briefest sight of her daughter as she rounded the corner of the cottage, lugging the small stump.

By the time Mrs. Waters had set up the arrangement for Leslie to spend the rest of the afternoon with a young friend, who lived in the village, Steven Roberts was knocking at the door.

"Come in and let's get started," Mrs. Waters said as soon as she'd opened the door.

"I don't want any part of this, Mrs. Waters. I'm only twenty years old. She told me she's pregnant but I don't want to marry her. It'll ruin my life," the young man pleaded, but he knew it would be of no use.

"It won't ruin your life, just change it. You did have sex with her, didn't you?"

He dropped his head. "Yes, but I don't love her and the baby's not mine."

"Love has nothing to do with it, Steven. And I'm well aware it's not your baby. Remember when you had mumps as a wee lad and your mum brought you to me for medicine to help you feel better? Well, that ended any hope that you'd ever father a child. However, we have a need for the baby. Lives will be ruined and lost but you'll survive. That's more than Sarah will be able to say. Now, as much as you don't want to hear this, you're going to have to stop them leaving for Cornwall. I know we discussed doing this later in Sarah's term, but it can't be helped. They can't leave the village."

"Why are they going to Cornwall all of a sudden?" he asked.

"To get away. I had a meeting with the Demmings and told them Sarah was pregnant and her baby would be taken from her. Lady Willsdon is barren so the baby boy will be given to her, to raise as her own child. That will ensure the succession to the estate and protect the village. Also, since you don't want any part of this baby, it lets you off the hook." She watched him as she said this, knowing that he understood he was far from being absolved.

"What am I to do, Mrs. Waters? They won't listen to me, especially Sarah. She's already told me I'm the only man she'll ever love, which is a lie, and is so daft she thinks I'll change my mind and marry her. If her dad thinks I got her pregnant, which I didn't, he'll throw me out of the house. I can't stop them from leaving."

"Yes, you can. And you're the only one to do it. After all, you are partly responsible for creating this situation. Sarah asked you to marry her, didn't she? To save face? And you've been having sex with her for a while, haven't you? Now, it's time you paid."

"How will I do it?" he said, fear making his voice shake.

"Murder."

Sarah answered the telephone on the first ring. "Demming residence," she said, a hopeful tone in her voice.

"Sarah, it's me."

"I knew you'd call, Steven. I knew you'd come back to me. I love you so much. We can talk about names for our baby. I hope it's a boy and he looks just like his handsome daddy."

Steven sighed and shook his head, wondering again how he'd ever let himself get tangled up with the likes of this one. "Would you like to go to the cinema tonight, Sarah? I could meet you around seven."

"Oh, yes! I have wanted to see the American movie that's playing now. It's called 'A Summer Place,' and it's supposed to be ever so romantic. I read all about it in the *Sixteen Magazine* in the library. Steven, I love you so much and I'm so happy."

"Listen, Sarah, could you meet me in front of the theatre? I don't want to be around your house if your dad is there. I know he hates me."

Starry-eyed, Sarah tried to assure him that her father didn't hate anyone, especially his soon-to-be son-in-law. "What did you say, Steven, I didn't catch that?" she asked.

"I groaned," Steven muttered to himself. "Nothing, Sarah, I'll see you tonight."

He put down the phone and Mrs. Waters smiled at him. "Good job, Steven. Now, let's get the others involved."

She picked up the receiver and made several calls, telling each of them to come to her house immediately.

Within the hour, Mrs. Water's living room was filled with people. "It's time to set our plan in motion," she said to them, knowing there was much reluctance about what had to be done to the Demming family. "I know you don't want to do this, but we must. It's our lives that are at stake. Do you want the village to whither away?" None of them wanted that, so the solution to the problem was discussed in detail. By the time the meeting had ended, everyone knew what his or her job would be.

"Steven, please stay back. I want to talk to you a bit more," she whispered the comment to him as she ushered the others out the door.

Mrs. Waters turned to him and watched his already pale face turn a lighter shade. She smiled and he backed up, trying to remove himself from the force of her personality.

"Why are you so afraid of me, Steven?" knowing the answer already, she moved purposely toward him. "It's time you and I got to know each other better." Her eyes glittered and she began to unbutton the dark-colored blouse that she wore. She did it slowly, and then pulled the pins from her long, blonde hair so that it fell in a bright cascade around her shoulders. She could tell his fear was leaving and lust was taking its place. It had been a long time since she'd showed a young man her power. It was going to be a sweet afternoon. She was glad she'd arranged for Leslie to spend the night with her friend.

When Steven went to meet Sarah at the cinema at seven that evening, he was in a stupor. He'd never been in love before. Now he understood what Sarah had been babbling on about. Too bad it wasn't her he was in love with, though. Following each of Mrs. Water's instructions, he treated Sarah as if he loved her. All he did was imagine it was Mrs. Waters he was with, instead of the doltish young girl. He barely recalled the movie. When he tried to recount his actions of the evening later, all he could remember was the feel of her skin, the womanly smell, and the way her blonde hair brushed like silk against his bare chest. He knew that no matter whom he was with, no one would fill his heart and mind like Mrs. Waters.

When the movie ended, the cinema was crowded and Steven held Sarah's arm as they made their way through the lobby and out to his car.

"Would you like to go to the pub and get a bite to eat?" he asked politely as he opened the passenger door for her.

"Yes, please," she answered shyly. "You aren't even acting like yourself, Steven. Is everything all right?" The happiness shining out of her eyes made Steven look away. It was too painful to know what was going to happen to her. Even if he didn't love the lass, he didn't want harm to come to her. But in these matters, Mrs. Waters knew best. He helped Sarah onto the seat and closed the door.

He started the car and drove onto the road that led to the pub.

"You missed the turn, Steven. The pub is behind us," Sarah said, not all that concerned. Just to be with him, certain he would marry her now, was so heavenly that nothing could make her feel sad. The world was perfect.

"I thought we'd go out to the stones. I know how daft you are about them," he answered, a nervous tone in his voice.

"But you hate it. You've always told me you think it's ridiculous how I love to go there. It makes me feel safe, like I'm in the sanctuary of a church."

"I just thought you'd enjoy it, that's all, luv. Now, sit back and relax. It won't be long now."

"You called me 'luv.' You've never done that before, Steven. I like this new you."

Steven drove along the curved road and listened to Sarah babble. The night was clear; moon and stars shining brightly over Salisbury Plain, and they hadn't met another car. When they rounded the final corner and Stonehenge came into sight, she quieted.

Leaning forward for a better view, she said, "Something's not right, Steven. The stones aren't welcoming me tonight. What's happened?" Her eyes were large and luminous and reminded Steven of deer eyes as he pulled the trigger.

Chapter Two

Present Day

The black-and-white Border collie looked good in a top hat, rakish, with a sort of devil-may-care attitude and a sloppy grin. I recalled when I grew on the farm with my grandfather in Eastern Montana that he'd had many dogs that looked just like this one. He used them to herd the cattle that covered the rolling plains as far as you could see. He said Border collies were the smartest dogs in the world, much smarter than most people he knew.

This dog's name was Jazz and I wondered if it was because he created such beautiful music. I would imagine there'd be lots to howl at around here, near Stonehenge in southeastern England. I had driven to the grocery to pick up a few items for my rented cottage, which had a small kitchen area in it. According to a large sign near him inside the store, Jazz was helping raise funds for a local charity. Children were lined up to get their photos taken with the "dog in the hat." He loved being the center of attention and was enjoying all the small hands that rubbed and petted his soft, silky fur.

I made my way around the line of children and walked slowly up and down the aisles of the market. It was the same but different from what I was used to in Las Vegas. The huge grocery store I shopped in there had many of the same products I saw on the shelves here in England. It just felt and looked different. Maybe because the store was so narrow, with low ceilings, and everything was stacked in a somewhat haphazard manner. It bustled with activity. I heard the children's laughter as they had their photos made with Jazz. I was charmed by all of it.

"Are you the new renter for Maple Cottage?"

I had my back turned to the man who asked the question but his voice sounded like he should work for the BBC.

I turned to face him and tried to hide my surprise. He was in a wheelchair and had his hand out to shake mine. "Rodney Willsdon, at your service. I'm also your landlord," he added. His face was ruddy, like he spent a good deal of time outdoors. He looked muscular and in top physical condition, at least from the waist up. His pant legs were empty from the knees down, the extra material tucked underneath him. Dark hair, in a short, military-style cut, and bright blue eyes made his white-toothed grin even more engaging.

"Is that how you know who I am?" I put a can of pork and beans back on the shelf and then shook his hand.

"It was a guess on my part. The agency told me you were an attractive redhead, very petite in stature. You fit the bill. Eva May Scott is your name, I believe?"

"Yes, it is, but please call me May. I did the paperwork for the cottage on-line. I suppose I thought the agency owned it, as well as renting it out to people who want to disappear for awhile."

He put his hands in his lap and looked at me quizzically. "What are you running away from?"

"Myself, mostly. But it's my ex-husband's fault I'm here. He wouldn't leave me alone."

"Hmm. What a topic of conversation amongst the canned goods. You must come by this afternoon for tea around four. Can you make it? I live in, forgive me for saying this, 'the big house,' also known as 'the pile,' behind the cottage. It sounds like one of your American expressions about a prison, doesn't it?"

I laughed. I liked this man. "I'll be there. Should I call you Rodney or Landlord?"

"Rodney will do. See you at four." He used what looked like a joystick to maneuver the wheelchair expertly through the small market aisles.

I continued to make my way slowly through the store, picking up items I thought I couldn't live without. Most of them were American. I should try new items instead of buying the same old things, I thought to myself as I inspected labels.

Dan, my ex-husband, was the main reason I found myself in this English village, centered between Stonehenge, Glastonbury and Amesbury. The day he called me at work and said he was on his way to visit from Tacoma, Washington, I knew I had to leave Las Vegas. Within twenty-four hours, I'd turned in early retirement paperwork from my job as a detective with the Las Vegas Metro Police, found and rented the cottage on-line, asked my friend Janet to take care of my cat, Whiskers, and got on a non-stop jet for London.

"Excuse me, please, Miss," a voice said politely. "Could I trouble you to move that way?" he asked as he pointed left with his finger. "I wanted to re-stock these shelves, if you wouldn't mind."

"Of course. I'm mostly browsing anyway."

"Do I detect an American accent?" he said as he began to put boxes of toothpaste onto the shelves.

"Yes, from Las Vegas."

"Ah! The Disneyland for adults; I've always wanted to visit. It's hot there, isn't it?"

"Yes, it can be very hot. In all kinds of ways."

"My name is Steven Roberts. Welcome to England and my grocery. It won't be as exciting as Las Vegas in our little village, but I'm sure you can find much to entertain you," he said, smiling. He reminded me of a tall, slightly overweight Santa. His pink-cheeked round face was pleasant. Thinning blond hair and glasses that kept sliding down his nose made him seem bumbling. There was, however, a gleam in his eyes, as he looked me over, in that predatory way that males think females never notice.

"I'm glad to be here and I'm sure I'll enjoy my stay." What I wanted was peace, quiet, bucolic surroundings, and rest.

He continued to stock the shelves and waved a cheery good-bye as I headed toward the front of the market and the registers.

I stood in line behind a harried mother with two small children in tow. "They never have both registers open and it's always a queue," she complained to whoever wanted to listen. The small boy, who looked to be about two, pulled on his mother's hand and begged for candy. She had a baby in a carrier on top of the grocery cart, which was mini-sized compared to American standards.

"Could I help you push the cart?" I asked, wanting to prevent the baby from toppling onto the floor.

"That's sweet, but I'm used to this. I'm just more run ragged today than usual." The young woman brushed a strand of lank brown hair off her face. "Whoever said motherhood isn't a full time job should try it sometime," she said.

"Your children are beautiful."

Her face lit up. "I know. I love to complain but I've got the world's best job. You're a tourist then?"

"Yes. I've rented Maple Cottage for a few weeks."

"Part of Lord Willsdon's pile. He's a nice chap. My husband, Bruce, went to elementary school with him, but was a few years younger than his nibs. Lord Willsdon got shipped off to a posh boarding school. Was a football star, too. Then he got his legs shot off in Northern Ireland. Never let it slow him down, though."

"I'm having tea with him this afternoon. He was in here a little while ago, which is how I met him and found out he's my landlord."

Her little boy clung to her legs and she dragged him along as the line moved like fudge toward the registers, both of which had opened. She cooed to the baby then turned back to me. "You'd never know Rodney was a 'lord' of anything. In fact, he and my Bruce are still the best of friends. Bruce does 'odds and ends' jobs for him sometimes. Did you say you were renting Maple Cottage?"

"Yes."

"Have you seen her?"

"Who?" I asked.

"Sarah."

"Does she live on the estate, too?"

"Well, she did until they found her body in a pool of her own blood, lying on the bathroom floor. Had a knitting needle up her."

"A botched abortion?" A horrible picture had formed in my mind.

"She was sixteen. It was the town scandal." She pushed the cart forward and prodded her son to move along. "The owner of this market was the father, but he wouldn't marry her."

"You mean that man who looks like Santa Claus?"

She laughed. "Steven does resemble Old Saint Nick, doesn't he? He was quite the looker when he was young. All that Viking blood, you know."

"Didn't the Vikings rape and pillage?"

"Like I said, he was the father."

"And she lived in Maple Cottage, where I'm staying?"

"Yes, that's why I wondered if you'd seen her. Lots of people have seen her over the years. She haunts the place. Sarah is our local 'claim to fame' and tourist attraction. I'm not scaring you, am I?" she asked innocently.

The hairs were standing up on the back of my neck and I felt chilled. "No," I lied. "I love the idea that I'm living in a haunted house."

We continued to creep forward. When it was her turn to unload the small cart she said, "My name is Amy Foster, by the way. I live on Barnstable Way. Come by for tea some afternoon. Anytime after three is fine."

"I'm May Scott and I'll take you up on your offer. I want to hear more about the ghost."

Amy pulled a notebook out of her purse and scribbled on a piece of paper.

"Here's my address and number. I'll look forward to your visit. Call and I'll give you directions so you won't get lost. Of course this place is so small that would be hard to do, wouldn't it? It'll be nice to have an adult conversation for a change. My mum knows all about Sarah, so we can have a good gossip about the village scandal, if you'd like."

I purchased a string bag to carry my few grocery items when I made it to the register. Everything here was done on a smaller scale and I had a lot to learn about local customs. Of course, that's part of the reason I came to England. When I was a child, I remember listening to my mother and grandmother as they talked about our English roots. After what I'd gone through over the past few months, leaving Las Vegas seemed like a wise move. Dan was the excuse I'd used to leave, but there were other memories that haunted me. Space and time were precious to me and I liked the feeling of anonymity as I walked the short distance to my rented Land Rover. I had to think a minute before I realized that I'd have to get in the passenger side to drive home. Driving on the left side of the road while sitting on the right was going to take some getting used to, and so far I hadn't done it very well. I'd almost turned the car back in and asked for a taxi service at Heathrow Airport a couple of days ago. I was used to racing along with ease on the long, empty stretches of highway in the Nevada desert. England's small roads, roundabouts and trucks, called lorries, that barreled along taking up too much space made me nervous.

"Could I be of assistance?" a deep male voice said, bringing me out of my reverie.

I turned and looked up at a tall middle-aged man in a dark brown suit, blindingly white shirt and somber tie.

"I got lost in my thoughts, but I'm also wondering how to get the car out of this tight parking space." Since I'd been inside the grocery, I'd been hemmed in front and back. "Parallel parking has always been difficult for me, and with the steering wheel being on the right and driving on the left side of the road, it's really a challenge," I said.

"My name is Paul Johnston, part of the local police establishment, and I'm at your service. Why don't you get in and I'll help you maneuver out of here? We want to keep our American tourists happy," he said.

With his help, I managed to get onto the road with little trouble. I gave him a quick wave and got into the traffic and headed for the cottage.

Chapter Three

Since it was so close to the village I determined that the next shopping trip would be on foot. I pulled in next to a yew hedge and turned off the engine with relief.

I'd picked the cottage from the web site because the photos were so charming. The roof was thatched and the exterior had a fresh coat of whitewash. Flowers of every color and size ran riot in the tiny garden plot. The River Avon meandered in the distance. I was close enough to have a slight view of it from the kitchen window and my goal was to sit along the banks at least twice each day. I gathered up my string bag of purchases and walked to the front door, managing to get it unlocked and myself inside without dropping anything.

Maple Cottage was fully furnished so all I had to provide was the food and personal items. I hadn't slept the first night. Maybe it was the time difference or nerves as I got used to my very different surroundings. I especially missed my cat, Whiskers, and thought again that it was a mistake to leave her with my friend Janet. The British quarantine laws were strict, though, and I didn't think it would have been fair to put her though that process.

It took a few minutes to put away my purchases. Then, like being drawn by a magnet, I went and looked at the bathroom floor. I wished Amy had never told me about the young girl's body that had been found lying there in a pool of blood so many years ago.

What I didn't want to think about was death. A serial killer had targeted Harvey Jordan, my former partner and mentor from the Tacoma, Washington, Police Department, his wife, and several other people; I was to be the cherry on top of the cake, so to speak. It was the last case I would ever work as a homicide detective. So why was I standing here staring at the floor?

I went back into the kitchen and thought about making coffee but realized it was almost time for me to walk to the "big house" for tea with my landlord. Since I'd never been much of a tea person, this was going to take some getting used to.

The telephone made a horrible jangling noise and I jumped. It was the first time it had rung since I'd arrived. "Hello?" I said into the bulky receiver. For some reason it was placed on top of the mantle with the cord dangling down in front of the fireplace. I'd have to find another place for it.

"Is that you, May?" asked a male voice.

"Yes, who is this?"

"You don't recognize your partner's voice?"

"Ed? You don't sound like yourself. Must be all the water and land between us."

"I had a little bird tell me you'd turned in paperwork to retire. Are you nuts? Why did you do that?"

"Because it's time for me to find something else to do with my life. I'm tired of chasing killers, and being chased in return."

"I know you went through a bad time, May, but you're the best partner I've ever had. Don't retire. Take a break and come back to work."

"That's kind of you to say that but you and I both know I drove you crazy. You're better off with Brenda." I smiled and tried not to chuckle. I knew he'd get tired of her endless sunny nature. She was so positive it was irritating.

"Brenda is boring. I miss you never doing anything by procedure. It made my life exciting."

"Oh, please. You're making me gag. You have been around Brenda too long. You've picked up her perky attitude." I checked my watch to see how long before I had to walk to Rodney's large house.

"Okay, maybe I exaggerate. But I do miss you. How's England?"

"Interesting, a little scary, especially the driving. I feel like a fish out of water. But I did this to myself, didn't I? You kept telling me to drive down to the Grand Canyon for a few days. I'm about to go have tea with my landlord."

"You don't like tea."

"This will be one more opportunity for me to change my negative attitude. Anyway, I heard a rumor that being negative will give you wrinkles, and I certainly don't need any more of those." I glanced in the mirror hanging over the mantle and looked at the crow's feet on each side of my eyes. "It may be too late in my case."

"Listen, I just wanted to check on you and see if this phone number you gave me actually worked. Call me sometime and let me know what you're up to. You went thorough hell and it'll take time for you to get over it. Everybody says hello and your boyfriend keeps asking if he should come over there."

"No, I don't want men around. I'm sick of all of you. I've had it. I'll never have anything else to do with anybody of your gender." It was fun to say and a total lie.

"I'll tell him not to get on any planes anytime soon. Listen, there's another reason I called and you're not going to like it."

"Has something happened to Whiskers? I know Janet took her, but it was reluctantly."

"No, your cat is fine. Your ex-husband called and I told him where you are and gave him your number."

"What did you say?"

"You heard me, May. I know I shouldn't have but Dan sounded so pitiful. I felt sorry for the guy."

"And you're a homicide detective who knows he's a crazy man who's stalking me," I sputtered.

"Yeah, but I know how are you are, too."

"What's that supposed to mean? I thought you wanted me to come back and be your partner again."

"I do, but Dan does care about you, May, even if he is a louse."

"You always did like him, but that's no reason you should have given away my hiding place."

"You don't think he'd come way over there, do you? I could see him coming to Las Vegas. But England? Come on, he won't do that," he said, trying to dig himself out of the hole he'd dug.

"You don't know the depths he'll go to. Look, I know you don't think you did anything that bad, but you did," I said, not wanting to let it go.

"Yeah, my wife told me I was screwed when I told her what I'd done. She said you'd be coming through the line to kick my butt, which you are."

"Smart wife you've got. Listen, if Dan shows up over here, I'm holding you totally responsible. Got it?"

"Got it."

"Perfect. Thanks for letting me know, Ed, and all the best to your family. Tell everybody I miss them. That doesn't include Dan, though." I held the receiver in my hand for a few seconds after he'd hung up. I had been rash in coming to England in such an abrupt manner. "Running away," is what my friend Janet had said I was doing.

I moved the ugly black phone from the mantle to a small table sitting next to the sofa. I hadn't really looked that closely at the room but now that I did I knew I was going to ask Rodney if I could rearrange the furniture. The first thing I wanted to find out was where the electrical plugs were located so I could move the sofa away from the beautiful bay window that it partially covered.

"Hmm. Hmm"

I stopped what I was doing and listened. It was quiet so I went back to my search.

"Hmm. Hmm" Was I hearing things now that I knew this cottage was haunted?

It sounded like scratching at the front door along with another couple of "hmm, hmms."

I got up off the floor, where I'd been searching for an outlet and tiptoed to the door. Leaning my ear against it, I heard nothing, then definitely another scratch. I peeked through the peephole to see if someone was on the steps. No one was there but I heard another definite scratch and this time a big, loud bark.

I was so surprised I jumped back, my heart racing. I'd come all this way for peace and quiet and instead I was on a high adrenaline rush, every nerve and hair standing at attention. My eyes felt big enough to pop out of my head. I stepped forward and opened it about an inch.

Jazz stood there, a big grin on his handsome face, waving his right paw at me. I walked onto the covered porch and he sat down politely. I did what he expected and petted him. It'd been such a long time since

31

I'd been around a dog that it almost seemed like I was committing some sort of betrayal, what with Whiskers waiting for me back in Las Vegas. My heart began to melt, though, and I knew I was a goner. I'd just told Ed no more males, and here I was not fifteen minutes later, captivated.

I squatted down, rubbed his ears, and scratched under his neck. When I did the same to his belly he rolled over onto his back with his paws in the air. I had a grand old time and so did he. I felt more peaceful than I had in months. I was in love. I hoped Jazz wouldn't break my heart, as most of his two-legged counterparts had done over the years.

"What's this around your neck, Jazz?" I said, noticing a small tube hooked to his collar.

"Woof," he said.

I sat back on my feet, in a yoga pose, and contemplated what he'd just told me.

"Woof," he repeated, and then rolled up into a sitting position. He waved his paw at me again and I finally got it.

"I'm supposed to open this?" I asked as I fingered the clear plastic tube.

He jumped around in delight and wagged his tail. He was getting me trained in a hurry and was proud of himself.

When he'd calmed down I took the cap off the tube and pulled out a piece of paper; "Jazz and I would like you to come to tea earlier than planned. If you can make it, he'll bring you to me. If not, tell him to go home and he will. Rodney."

I stood up and opened the door wide. "Come in while I get ready, Jazz."

He walked in behind me and took a seat in front of the hearth. I scurried around and checked my hair and lipstick. Both were about as good as they were going to get so I gave up and went back into the living room. I took the cottage key out of my purse and put it into my shirt pocket.

"Let's go to tea," I told my bright companion.

He led the way as I closed and locked the door behind me. We walked a short distance past the cottage to an open-gated entryway. The paved road, which was wide enough for one small car, was lined with tall trees. It looked like we were walking into a park. The road serpentined its way through the woods. Jazz trotted by my side, completely at home. He glanced up and grinned at me occasionally, as if to let me know he was proud of how fast I'd caught on to his instructions. I had no illusions as to who was in control.

We rounded a curve and suddenly a huge, gothic horror of a house loomed in front of me. I stopped and gaped in amazement. It looked like something Bela Lugosi or Boris Karloff would have lived in, at least in their movies. The only thing that saved the house from being totally repulsive was the gardens. Plants and flowers grew in wild abandon, and the clutter softened the dark-turreted stone house, making it approachable.

Jazz herded me away from the front door and around to the back. I followed as he padded to a door that was almost hidden by the riot of climbing roses that formed a graceful entryway. They had a spicy cinnamon smell and I stopped and stuck my nose in the closest one to me. They were multi-colored and reminded me of fireworks on the Fourth of July. Of course, that wouldn't be much of a holiday in England.

"You like the roses?" Rodney asked as he opened the wide back door and rolled onto the pathway. Jazz went immediately to his side and Rodney stroked him.

"I do. I also didn't know you belonged to Jazz. When I saw you at the market I didn't put the two of you together."

"Jazz and I have been together since his birth, haven't we, boy?" Rodney asked as he hugged the dog to him. "He comes from a long line of ancestral Border collies from the Scottish Highlands and has a higher pedigree than anyone in the village."

"He's so smart. Did he come that way or has he been trained?" I stayed under the arbor, unwilling to leave the beauty and smell of the exquisite roses.

"He has such an illustrious heritage that it didn't take much to train him. He did go to school to learn how to help me out. I couldn't live as well as I do if he wasn't here." Jazz and Rodney looked at each other and the love was palpable.

"Would you like to have tea in the garden?" Rodney asked.

"That would be delightful," I answered.

I followed Rodney and Jazz as we walked down a paved pathway to the far side of the house. The lawn ended at a small lake and the view was breathtaking. As ugly as the house was, someone had decided long ago to make up for it in the gardens.

"This place is magical," I said, looking in wonder at the manicured grass and huge trees.

"I've lived here all my life, so I guess I'm used to it," Rodney said and smiled. He expertly pulled his chair up to an umbrella-covered round table. "Take a chair, please, May."

I sat with my back to the house and gazed out at the lake. "Are those swans?"

"Yes, they belonged to my mother. When she passed away, I kept them. She did love them so," he commented wistfully.

"You live here alone?" I hoped I wasn't being too nosy.

"Sort of. I have help in the house and for the grounds. There's no family, though. My parents have both passed away. They're buried in the town cemetery, just over the hill." He pointed to a small hill that rose up behind the lake. "I like to think they look out for me," he said.

"That's the way I am, too. No parents or brothers and sisters, either."

"I guess that makes us middle-aged orphans," he said and smiled at me. Jazz lay next to the wheel of his chair, head resting on his front paws.

Chapter Four

After I returned to the cottage I took a nap. Something about the time changes between here and Las Vegas made me sleepy. I felt sure that after I awoke things would take on a rosy perspective. I kept having a vague uneasiness about my trip and being so far from home. I wasn't ready to admit that it had been a mistake to "run away," as my friend Janet had told me I was doing. I wanted this journey to heal me, not make me sad that I wasn't with my friends or my cat, Whiskers.

I thought about building a house in Pahrump, since I now had over fifty acres of land in that arid high desert area, sixty miles west of Las Vegas. Thanks to my mentor and friend Harvey, who had been murdered almost a year ago, I owned real estate in Nevada and Washington State. I couldn't shake the fact that he and his wife, Stephanie, were gone. Their deaths made me a wealthy woman. Harvey had left his considerable estate to me, his "daughter of choice, not circumstance," as he'd said in his will. I still felt guilty about the inheritance. Money wasn't something I'd ever wanted or had gone after in my life. And here I was, rich, but at what price?

Of course, that was the key motivation behind Dan's sudden interest in me. He'd never met a dollar he didn't love and eventually squandered.

I slept longer than I wanted but indeed felt much better when I awoke. The sun was waning in the sky and I decided to do something I'd dreamed of doing since I'd first heard of the place in junior high back in Montana– watch Stonehenge merge into the dark shadows as the sun set.

I scurried around the cottage and put together a small picnic supper so I could take advantage of the natural otherworldly shows I was about to enjoy. I managed to drive on the left side of the road and make it without incident to the megalithic site, which took less than twenty minutes. In a way the treeless Salisbury Plain reminded me of parts of Nevada and Montana; the endless sky converging with the brownish-green rolling hills. I was beginning to enjoy myself immensely when I rounded a curve and came upon my first view of Stonehenge – and the hundreds of cars and busses that were parked at some distance from the stones. I'd read this was the most-visited place in England, but I had no idea it would be like this. I slowed and pulled off the road. A fence surrounded the stones and I understood the precaution.

Even with the scores of people and the fences, the enormous stones were unbelievable in their grandeur and the power they conveyed. During my conversation with Rodney he'd mentioned something about the influx of tourists during the summer solstice, so perhaps that's what this was all about. According to him, hundreds of people camped out as near to the stones as they were allowed to follow whatever rituals their beliefs required.

I pulled far enough off the road to feel safe getting out of the car. I walked a short way up the hill next to the car and spread a blanket on the rocky ground. There was no way I was going to go any closer to the stones, not this time at least. I brought out my small meal and watched from a distance as people flowed around the sacred site. As the sun faded, campfires began to dot the landscape. They looked like fireflies flickering in the twilight that had settled on Salisbury Plain. The stones seemed to glow, perhaps emitting the heat from the sun. Sounds caught my attention and I realized that some of the groups were chanting, singing, and although they made different music, they blended in a discordant harmony. I shivered, not so much from the cool evening air, but from being in this strange place with people I had no connection to and no knowledge of their traditions. What did they want the stones to do for them? Could the stones provide respite from whatever pain they felt? Too many unanswered questions and the ground had quickly gotten cold and hard. I gathered up my few items, stowed them in the car, and drove back to the cottage.

* * *

I thought I was dreaming. No one could possibly want to get up on a cold, rainy morning like this. I rolled over and pulled the warm covers over my head. Unfortunately, the knocking got louder. "Miss Scott, are you in there?" yodeled a pleasant though aggravating voice.

I pulled the covers off one eye and looked at the clock; 6:30 a.m. What was wrong that I had to awaken so early? Surely the pubs weren't open at this time. Giving up, I arose, put on my robe and blearily made it to the front door. "Who's there?" I asked, not unlike one of the three little pigs.

"I'm so sorry to disturb you, Miss. I'm Mrs. Long, Mr. Rodney's housekeeper."

I unlocked and opened the heavy door. "Please come in, Mrs. Long. Is something wrong?" This couldn't be good. I hoped nothing had happened to Rodney or Jazz.

"Oh, everything is fine. But he wanted to ask if you'd like to accompany him to his office today. He works at the Shrivenham Campus of Cranfield University, near Swindon," Mrs. Long was beyond middle-aged, and "pleasingly plump," as my mother used to say of her friends who were slightly overweight. "I tried to ring you up but got no response." She walked in and looked where the phone had been placed, before I'd moved the furniture around. "It seems that your line is unplugged," she said, as she pointed to the line, still lying on the back of the couch. Her expression let me know I shouldn't have done that.

I must have forgotten to plug it back in when I shifted a few pieces of furniture around. "Yes, he told me a little bit about his job with the university yesterday. It sounds fascinating." I walked to the couch and plugged the phone in the outlet.

"After you left yesterday he tried to call, but I guess you'd gone out or perhaps the phone was out of commission by then."

"I took a drive to Stonehenge. I didn't realize it would be mobbed with so many visitors. Would you like coffee, Mrs. Long?" I was beginning to long for a strong cup, maybe several of them.

"No, thanks. As for the tourists, it's the solstice due in a few days. It brings the crazies out of the woodwork," she said as she stepped back outside. "Shall I tell Mr. Rodney you'll accompany him today?"

"Yes, please. What time will he leave?"

She laughed. "In about an hour, I'm afraid."

"No problem. I can be ready by then." First, though, I would put the coffee on to brew while I showered. My friend Janet's husband, a career Air Force officer, had advised me to take a coffee pot, with the current converter on the end, and several cans of coffee to England. It's a wonderful country, but coffee isn't their forte.

"He'll pick you up here. It's a pleasure to meet you, Miss Scott. It's so refreshing not to have some dowdy old couple renting the cottage. You'll add some life to the place I'm sure."

"Thank you. So far, I've enjoyed it." It was only a little white lie. "Before you go, Mrs. Long, could I ask you a question?"

"Why of course," she answered, folding her hands primly in front of her.

"I've been told this cottage is haunted. Is that true?"

Mrs. Long looked down at her feet, then up as though a Michelangelo fresco covered the low ceiling. Finally, she looked at me. "Have you seen Sarah?"

"No, but I've heard about her. Can you tell me her story?" I asked. "Come in and sit down – I have enough time before Rodney will arrive. That is, if you have a few minutes you can spend with me." I motioned toward the small sofa and she joined me as I sat down.

"It was so long ago," she began, "I don't know how much is truth and how much is lost in legend. I've tried for all these years since to put it out of mind, like it never happened. Sarah was a beautiful young girl, so full of life. I know she gave her mum and dad fits, but she was a kind-hearted creature. Nothing made her sad. She was truly like a beam of sunshine in all our lives. I think that's why we could never let Sarah go," Mrs. Long said. She looked down at her hands. "I was so young myself, back then."

"Did she die in the cottage bathroom?" I asked, trying not to see the image of her bloody body on the small tiled floor. "That's what Amy Foster told me yesterday when I met her at the village market."

"Supposedly she does haunt the cottage-that's how the tourist bit started," Mrs. Long commented, not answering my question. "Sometimes I feel guilty that the village has turned her death into a money maker. Times were different in the sixties. You're too young to know about it, but there was a different feel. It was like part of us were moving forward into the new times, but some of the villagers didn't want to let go of the old ways."

I looked at her with interest. "Old ways?"

"You have to understand where you are. We live with the legends of Merlin, the Lady of the Lake on the Isle of Avalon and of course, Stonehenge. To some of us, those were not fairy tales but part of our lives. It's not so much that way now. Sarah got caught up in the old ways, I'm ashamed to say. My favorite memory of her is just a little while before she died. Her parents were moving away, to get her away from the prying eyes of the village."

I shifted so I could look directly at her. "Is that because she was pregnant?"

"Yes, in those days, unlike now, if a girl got pregnant before marriage, her life was ruined, and that of her family, too." She stood up and said, "I do need to get back now."

I knew I'd got as much information as I could, at least for the moment. I shut the door and locked it after she left, then headed for the kitchen to make a quick cup of coffee.

Chapter Five

I went into the bathroom, showered, toweled off and combed my hair. The mirror was foggy so I grabbed a hand towel and rubbed the glass. That seemed to make it worse so I added a little water to the towel and went back at it with a vengeance.

As I stared into the mirror four eyes looked back and only two of them were mine. I rubbed my eyes and peeked through my fingers, not wanting to see what appeared to be a pale female face. Her eyes were the saddest I'd ever seen. I turned quickly to speak to her but she wasn't there. It felt as though a cold wind had blown through the small room, and I shivered. "Who was that?" I asked out loud, knowing it was Sarah.

I left the bathroom and did a slow walk through the cottage. All I wanted was peace and quiet, not a ghost hunt. I dressed quickly and went outside to wait. Looking back at the small cottage, nothing seemed unusual. I half expected to see the face hovering behind a curtain, waiting for me to leave.

Rodney pulled up in a Chevrolet Suburban. I couldn't imagine that a vehicle that large could fit easily on the roads.

"Okay, what's the secret? How do you keep one of Detroit's finest on these narrow highways?" I asked as I climbed onto the running board and sat down in the huge SUV. "I can barely get the Land Rover to fit and it was made for these roads, wasn't it?"

"Yes, it was, but I'm used to maneuvering. And this rig is perfect for hauling my chair around," he responded as he expertly drove the car using his hands. There were pedals, too, but everything could be operated by hand controls and he had it down to an art.

Jazz sat between us on the bench seat. Soon he moved next to me and put his head on my lap. He smiled up at me with those beautiful brown eyes.

"I love this dog," I cooed to no one in particular. My hands moved over his silky coat and I scratched under his neck. He paid me with soft dog kisses on my hands. "And you love me, don't you, Jazz?" He wriggled and looked up at me adoringly.

Rodney laughed. "He has all the luck with the girls."

"Speaking of girls, I just met one in the bathroom mirror. She had the saddest eyes I've ever seen. Who's the ghost that's living with me in the cottage?" I watched for a reaction but it was more than I expected.

Rodney almost wrecked his beloved Suburban.

Jazz managed to stay on the seat even as the huge vehicle swerved across the road. I grabbed him and hung on, as if he could protect me from what I knew was going to be a head-on crash with another car or one of the huge trees that were so close to the road. They were beautiful and created a canopy of green over many of the roads in England, but they could also be deadly.

Rodney pulled and pushed on the levers that controlled the car and managed to get it back in the left lane, but it did rock back and forth. He slowed the speed and we eventually came to a stop. He pulled off the berm onto a side road and sucked in deep breaths.

"I didn't mean to upset you so much, Rodney. Unless I imagined it, there was the face of a young woman in my bathroom mirror this morning. It freaked me out so I had to ask. Do you think its Sarah? Amy Foster told me Sarah haunted the place. Said her body was found in a pool of blood, lying on the bathroom floor. Is that who I saw, Rodney?"

He eased himself back in his seat and turned to face me. "I've heard stories but have never had the pleasure of meeting the ghost. I do apologize for that over-reaction. I can't think what made me lose control like that."

My years of police work took over and I began to look at Rodney in a whole new light. "There's certainly a lot of emotion surrounding the idea of Sarah haunting the place. It happened a long time ago, but for you it seems to be a fresh wound."

"One, apparently, that I can't forget. She's the village scandal, or saint, depending on who you talk to. It took place during my parent's time, so it's ancient history. They all knew each other. My mother took it upon herself to take care of Sarah's grave. Sarah's mum went bonkers after it happened and has been locked away these many years. I've heard stories but never took them seriously. And you saw her in the mirror?"

He said it in a straightforward manner that made it sound plausible. However, Amy had told me it was well known in the village that Steven Roberts had been the father of the baby that Sarah aborted. I wondered what sort of tales Rodney had heard and why they continued to upset him after such a long time had passed.

I rubbed Jazz's fur and enjoyed his warmth against my leg. "I lost my mentor and former partner to a murderer almost a year ago so I can understand how rumors can run rampant. I'm a good listener and would like to hear all the versions of this village scandal."

"Let's do that later. I want to get back on the road and be the tour guide I intended to be today. I want you to see where I work and be impressed by my expertise in military matters." He started the huge vehicle and we lumbered back onto the one-lane road.

Jazz, who had nodded off, woke up and moved closer to Rodney. Intelligent dog that he was, he knew who needed comforting. "Okay, we can talk later. We'll pass Stonehenge, won't we?" I knew the answer, but figured it would take his mind off Sarah.

The rest of the trip was uneventful. We spent about two hours at the Shivenham Campus, met a few of his colleagues and heard much more than I wanted to know about distance education and the military.

On the way back he suggested we stop at the P&P for lunch.

"P&P?" I asked, ready to try anything because I was starved.

"The Prince and Pauper. It's my favorite pub. Do you like toad in the hole?"

"I have no idea. I'm so hungry I guess I could eat a toad. Is it fried frog legs?"

He laughed, "Oh, I guess you don't know what that is, do you? It's one of our 'guess what it is' foods like bubble and squeak or bangers and mash."

"I'll try anything once, as long as it's cooked. I'm not eating any sort of sushi frog, though. "

We took another road back to the village and this one was so narrow that the SUV took up the entire road. "What happens if we meet another car?' I asked with my hands tightly clenched. My body swayed from side to side as we wound around the curvy, sloped road. I was having an interior dialogue that went something like this: "I will not get carsick; I will not get carsick; I will not...."

Much to my delight, the P&P appeared around a curve and we pulled off the road and into a vacant space in the parking lot, the only one left.

"Ah, you've brought me luck. I usually have to park on the side of the road," Rodney commented as he expertly turned his seat around, and then maneuvered himself into his wheelchair. He made it look effortless. The motor whirred as the door slid open and a ramp lowered so he could roll down the slight incline to the paved surface.

"Can we bring Jazz with us?" I asked, as the dog nimbly jumped down from the high bench seat.

"Of course; he's a regular." Rodney rolled toward the ivy-framed entrance. The pub was a half-timbered two-story building. Small thick-paned windows had flower boxes hooked to the front. Petunias and geraniums spilled out and over in a rainbow of colors.

The massive wooden door creaked as Rodney pushed it open and I followed him and Jazz into a dark interior that was alive with noise. It took a moment for my eyes to adjust to the gloom.

"Well, look what the cat's dragged in," a woman said. She was behind the mammoth bar and the brightest thing in the room the white-blonde hair that formed a halo around her face.

She walked around the end of the bar and Jazz went into a frenzied delight as she rubbed him behind his ears and spoke in a quiet voice. Whatever she said made him grin and he licked her hands. "This dog loves Guinness," the woman said. She was petite, middle-aged and dressed like the hookers I used to see walking around the back streets of the Fremont District. A skirt barely covered her rounded behind and fishnet stockings covered shapely legs. Ample breasts oozed from the top of a skin-tight pink sweater. I didn't know how she could walk in her red-sequined stiletto heels. She left Jazz panting at her feet as she extended her small, delicate hand to me, "Leslie Waters Sumac, owner of the Prince and Pauper. It's a pleasure to meet you."

We shook hands, hers was still damp from dog kisses, and I mumbled an embarrassed, "Glad to meet you." I hope she hadn't been reading my mind.

I noticed that Rodney was enjoying this little scene immensely.

Obviously, I'd been the topic of conversation between these two already, so there was no telling what other little surprises they had waiting for me.

Rodney wheeled to a corner table, and Jazz trotted beside me as we joined him. The chair was heavy as I pulled it away from the small wooden table. Jazz made himself comfortable between us on the floor.

"The usual?" Leslie asked Rodney as she continued to check me out.

"Let's have two toads, please. And a couple of pints."

"I have a big, juicy bone for Jazz. Do you want him to have it now?" She reached down and patted his head.

"Why not? It's a party!" Rodney exclaimed.

"If you don't mind, I'd like a coffee instead of the pint. Not to be a party pooper, but I don't care for the taste of ale."

Jazz, Rodney, and Leslie looked at me as if I had insulted the Queen.

"You're from Las Vegas and don't like ale?" Leslie asked, her massive bosoms jiggling.

"My parents were killed by a drunken driver in Montana, so I never touch alcohol." I said it succinctly, but the pain still quivered inside of me. It had been years, but I'd never forgotten how lost I'd felt as I looked at their mangled bodies lying in the morgue. The idea of riding with Rodney, after he'd had his pint, wasn't making me feel very safe.

"Blimey, I'm sorry. Coffee it will be," she said, sashaying toward the bar and kitchen beyond.

"I should have asked first what you wanted," Rodney apologized.

"That's okay. I'd offer to drive us back, but I have no clue how to drive your car."

"Oh, you mean the pint? It will be all right. We're not that far from the village anyway. It's just over the next hill."

I thought, "That's what they all say." Out loud I commented that it seemed Leslie had a successful business.

"Yes, quite," he replied, with a distinctive grin.

"You look like you're just bursting to tell me something. What is it?" I queried.

"I've always thought that our Leslie is similar to that country singer you have in America. Dolly Parton, is her name, I believe. So much more to her than meets the eye, so to speak."

"I understand what you mean. Don't underestimate Dolly and Leslie.

They're smart cookies."

Jazz snored under the table.

"You can say that and get away with it. If I did, I'd be summoned by the nearest barrister."

The food came; I ate like a starved pig and thought I'd share the small bit I had left with Jazz. His nose had awakened him as soon as Leslie brought the steaming plates of sausages in a crust, gravy, mashed potatoes and peas. "Do you mind if I share with Jazz?" I asked Rodney.

"A little bit is okay but normally he doesn't eat off the table," he commented as he gave his dog a head scratch.

Jazz's head rested on my knees and he looked at me as if he'd never had a bite of food before; only some of the toad in a hole I had left on my plate would stop those brown eyes from looking so sad. I reached toward my plate; I saw the faintest thump of his tail. As I brought the food to his mouth, his tail was in full, furious wag. After the food was gone, Jazz continued to lick my fingers with his soft tongue. I grabbed his head and ruffled his ears.

"I say, wish I had Jazz's way with the girls," Rodney commented with a mock-sad look.

"You said that before. Both of you have the ability to make us want to give you your every wish and desire," I bantered back, still stroking Jazz's soft black-and-white coat.

"What did you say, luv?" Leslie asked as she swayed towards us on sexy stilettos. "Don't go giving him more airs than he's already got. He's too big for his breeches now, so be careful."

Rodney sat up straight in his wheelchair and said, "Nonsense! I'm the bravest fellow I know."

Leslie winked at me and said, "Good thing he's so cute. He gets away with murder, this one does. Can I get you some dessert, more coffee, another ale?"

"No," Rodney said, "that should hold us until dinner. Put it on my tab, will you?"

"It's already there. You three have fun. See you again soon, May?"

"Absolutely. I'm going to try the bubble and squeak next."

Rodney stopped and spoke to several men and women in the pub and managed to pet all the dogs that were with their owners. Finally, we made our way out to the van.

I stood back and watched as he got into the huge Suburban; Jazz followed close behind. I opened the passenger door on the left and sat on the big cushy seat.

The sun was shining brightly as we entered the English village. It reminded me of pictures I'd seen in the storybooks my mother used to read to me so long ago in Montana. I could almost hear her soft voice as she read the stories of King Arthur, Guinevere, Lancelot, Merlin, the Lady of the Lake, and the mystical Isle of Avalon, currently named Glastonbury.

"Our ancestors are from this part of England, May. Someday you'll visit and see how beautiful it is. I hope I can go with you, as my Mother did with me," she'd said.

Her wish didn't come true. I was alone in this lush English countryside. But her voice was clear from so far ago. She lived with me still, in my heart, and I knew she was glad to be a part of my journey.

Chapter Six

We pulled in front of the cottage and as I got out asked Rodney if I could take Jazz for a walk. "I'm so stuffed I need to burn some of that food off. I'll turn into a butterball, as short as I am, if I don't get some exercise."

"He'll love it. When you get back, just tell him to go home and he will." Jazz hopped down from the van and sat next to me, looking expectant. "See? He knows he's going for a walk," Rodney said as he waved and drove toward the long drive that led to his estate.

"Jazz, where do you want to go?" I knew full well that he had our walk all planned. Some people might find Border collies too controlling, but I loved their intelligent leadership. "I'll follow you, Boss," I said to him as he looked back at me, tongue lolling out of his mouth.

He walked slightly in front of me. We went through a lovely copse of trees that I knew would be exquisite when autumn came. I'd be back in Las Vegas by then and regretted that I wouldn't be able to see them in their colorful glory. I could imagine how the leaves would crunch underfoot as people walked along the paths.

The land was every conceivable shade of green. Birds twittered and flew around in the tops of the trees as we disrupted their quiet afternoon. We came to a large field and I heard a shrill whistle. Soon, over the top of a gentle knoll, sheep ambled toward an opening in a dilapidated fence that led to the village. A smaller version of Jazz rode herd on them. It amazed me that one dog could work so many animals at once, keeping them in line. The Border collie ran around and kept the baaing sheep together. Jazz and I watched from the edge of the trees as a tall, lanky man in blue denim pants held up by suspenders, a checkered shirt, and a wool cap on his head, came into view. He had a wooden staff in his right hand, but it was clear his dog was the leader of this parade.

As the dirty white sheep with black ears stopped to eat grass, turned in the wrong direction and ran into each other, the dog, with saint-like patience, nudged them through a wide opening in the fence and corralled them toward the town. I saw colorful clothes swaying in the breeze on a clothesline behind a gabled brick cottage. Beyond that the square church tower watched over the sleepy village. Two women, one leaning on a bicycle, talked at the end of the pavement. The sky had cottony clouds with a little peach pink in them. Wildflowers bloomed at the base of the trees where Jazz and I watched the pastoral scene.

"Let's walk to the church," I said. We made our way slowly, staying far enough behind the sheep that we didn't startle them. Jazz took me around to the back of a thicket and we proceeded toward the church. As we came in sight of it, there was a small graveyard to the right of the church, away from the main part of the village.

"Turn here," I said as I steered the dog in a different direction.

Some of the headstones were so old that the writing had all but disappeared. A small stone almost directly in the center caught my eye. I walked over and looked down at the inscription, which was still easy to read:

FOREVER OUR BELOVED DAUGHTER

Underneath the words was the name SARAH MARIE DEMMING, her birth and death date were listed. I did a quick calculation and realized she had died at sixteen. I hadn't been born when she died. This was the grave of the young woman who supposedly had killed herself in a botched abortion and now haunted the cottage that I rented. Had I intentionally made my way to her gravesite? Rodney had said that his mother had taken care of her grave, and that Sarah's mom had gone crazy with grief. I could understand that – if it hadn't been for my grandfather taking me under his wing, I don't know what would have happened to me after my parents' death.

Did Sarah's face appear to me in the mirror, or had I imagined it? What did her sad eyes want me to understand about her life and death? Maybe I could go into the village and read the old newspapers that must have been filled with stories of her death and, I hoped, a photo. The shops were still open, which meant the newspaper and library should be, too.

I looked around at the small graveyard and noticed a large mausoleum almost hidden by dense shrubbery. As I approached, the smell of the boxwood was overwhelming and I stopped to cover my mouth and nose. I hated this smell. It reminded me of exactly where I was – in a cemetery.

Jazz had taken a seat in a patch of sunshine and rolled around on his back, scratching. I'd have to make sure to brush his fur before sending him home to Rodney. I walked toward the opening of the crypt and pushed open the rusted iron gate. It was at least twenty degrees cooler within the thick stonewalls and I shivered. Large marble coffins ringed the room. I made my way to what looked like the newest, read the plaque on top, and saw that it was Rodney's mother who rested there. His dad was next to her, plus other relations who made up the village aristocracy from hundreds of years ago. I felt sorry for Rodney because he must be destined to spend eternity in this desolate place. I couldn't wait to get back outside, even with the awful smell of the boxwood.

Jazz and I walked into the village and the sunshine felt wonderful on my skin. I looked up at the sky and involuntarily shivered, thinking of the sarcophaguses just a few steps away.

I found the library first and told Jazz to wait outside for me. He promptly took a seat under a rhododendron bush. A bell tinkled when I pushed the glass-paned door open.

An older woman was behind a counter and her glasses were perched halfway down her nose. "Could I help you?" she inquired pleasantly.

"Yes, please. I'd like to know where to start to locate information on a young girl who died in the village in 1965."

"Ah, you're the summer renter for Lord Willsdon's cottage and you've seen the ghost," she said, as if this was a usual occurrence.

"Yes, I have. At least I think I saw something. Other people have seen her, too, then, as I've been told?" The library was small but welcoming.

"Oh, quite. Sarah is our claim to fame around here. It's interesting how she went from being the town scandal to our heroine. Ghost hunters travel here to visit the cottage and the cemetery. She's our glamour girl, so to speak."

"Mrs. Long told me a little bit about her. Is there a photo of Sarah or an article from the newspapers when she died that I could look at?" I asked.

"We printed a little pamphlet about her some years back, when her ghost kept appearing at such regular intervals. She only appears, though, to women. Did you know that? However, I'm not sure if I still have one of the pamphlets," she said.

"That's okay; I'm getting used to the idea that I've rented a real haunted English cottage."

"Your name is May Scott, I believe? Amy Foster told me about you after you two chatted at the grocery. She's expecting you to come to tea. I'm Joan Pritchard, by the way. I married George, one of Sarah's cousins."

"It's a pleasure to meet you, Mrs. Pritchard. Do you believe the story about the botched abortion?" I figured the townsfolk, especially a relative, had the sordid details down pat by this time.

"I went to school and church with Sarah. She and I played together as children. No, I really don't know what happened, other than the stories about her and Steven. He's always denied he got her pregnant, and he never left the village. I guess that's his way of proving his innocence – by not leaving," she said, and then continued. "I recall that she had a crush on a young man who worked at the manor house-looked a bit like that American actor, James Dean. Didn't he die in a car accident?" she asked, as she wiped a speck of imaginary dust off the counter.

"He did. Who was the young man she had a crush on?"

"I can't remember his name but he had the biggest gold skull ring I've ever seen, then or since. He could have used that thing for a weapon," Mrs. Pritchard said. "Got it when he was in the Navy and was stationed in Hong Kong."

"Does he still live around here?"

She smiled and shook her head, "No, he was a drifter. Sarah did like him, though. But then, Sarah liked all the boys, if you know what I mean."

I thanked her for the information and walked onto the street, closing the door behind me. I kneeled down next to Jazz and gave his head and ears a rub.

It was a sad but intriguing story, but one with no firm truth to it. Obviously lives had been lost and changed because of the events from so long ago, but what were the true facts behind it, I wondered.

Maybe that explained why Sarah's ghost hadn't left the cottage. Perhaps she was trying desperately to get someone to listen to her and finally solve the mystery of her death. If you believed in psychics, which I didn't, they'd say that was precisely what she was trying to do.

It had been a long time since her death and the village had turned it into a moneymaking venture.

The tale was sordid enough the way it was. It made me wonder, though, if it was even worse. Maybe the young girl hadn't tried to abort a baby at all; perhaps she had been murdered.

Sighing, I decided that what I needed to do was to mind my own business and enjoy my stay in this ancient and beautiful country.

Chapter Seven

Jazz and I continued our walk through the village. I looked into display windows and almost went into the shoe shop to try on a pair of summer sandals that enticed me. I turned away, thinking I couldn't afford what they cost when it dawned on me for yet another time that I no longer had to worry about money. I was so used to doing without, though, that I couldn't bring myself to go into the shop and spend so much on shoes. Going from a detective's salary to a wealthy woman's bottomless checking account wasn't easy for me and I still felt guilty about it. I'd much rather have Harvey, his wife and the others who had been murdered than the material things that I'd inherited.

The newsagent's shop was closed for the day but I would make a point to walk over in the morning and try to locate the pamphlet that Mrs. Pritchard mentioned. Maybe they had a copy of it or a photo of her. I had formed a picture of Sarah in my mind's eye, based solely on what I thought I saw in the bathroom mirror. It would be interesting to find out if what I saw was how Sarah looked back in the mid-sixties.

I hadn't realized it but I had walked to the door of the grocery. Steven Roberts was working one of the registers. I told Jazz to sit and he did immediately. I walked up to the door and it swung open. The grocery looked the same as the first time I'd come in, except it wasn't filled with kids having their photo made with Jazz. I'd have to ask Rodney how much money he'd raised for charity.

I pushed a small basket around, trying to stay near the front so I could unobtrusively observe Steven as he worked in the market. He cheerfully waited on the customers and seemed to give special attention to attractive women. I guess the old saw about the leopard never changing its spots applied to Steven. I put a few items in my cart and stood in line behind a burly guy who looked to be buying his lunch. He cast a glance my way but didn't engage me in conversation. I'd been told the English weren't especially open to foreigners, at least until they got to know them. From my perspective, they'd been very friendly. I'd figured having Rodney as my landlord was the reason for my easy acceptance. Amy Foster had certainly been open with me the day I'd stood in line behind her in this market. I should ring her up and visit, as she'd invited. But as I thought about it, maybe she'd been too friendly.

I shook my head to bring myself back to reality. I was turning this entire visit into an investigation and had gotten to the point that I didn't believe or trust anyone; except Jazz, that is.

After I purchased the few items, we took our time walking back to the cottage. The village was filled with late afternoon shoppers and their string bags, tourists and their cameras. As I walked along I heard several languages being spoken, some of which I recognized. The shoe shop window with the beguiling sandals beckoned me again. This time I went inside. Jazz promptly lay down next to the door and settled in for another nap.

The bell tinkled my arrival as I pushed the door open but the shop was empty. I set my string bag on the floor and took the pair of sandals from the window display. The size looked like it should fit me so I sat on a brightly colored, chintz-covered chair to take my tennis shoes off and try them on. I looked around and called "Hello?" but no one answered.

The sandals felt wonderful on my feet and I took a walk around the small room to test them. There was a bell on the counter so I walked over and rang it. The opening that led to the back of the shop was covered by a curtain that hung from what looked like a pressure mount shower curtain rod; just like the one I had at my house in Las Vegas. I looked around the room once more, then gingerly stepped behind the counter and pulled the curtain open as I called "Hello?" again. It ran through my mind that I must be breaking many English laws as I nosily scanned the cluttered back room. No one was there but I thought I heard faint voices. I walked into the room and noticed a stairway that hadn't been in view from where I'd been standing. I put my hand on the rail and tentatively put one sandaled foot on the bottom step. The voices were coming from the room behind the closed door at the top of the stairs. I had a short discussion with myself about the error of doing this and then slowly moved up the stairs. At the top I tiptoed to the door, leaned my ear against it and listened to the now heated conversation. Raised voices shouted out accusations about money being mishandled and another voice, female, tried to pacify them. "It was done for our protection, you know that. We talked about it in this very room. We must keep going or our village will die."

After all the efforts by Ed and Harvey, my former partners, to instill proper police procedural methods, here I was sticking my nose in where it certainly didn't belong. All I wanted was to buy the shoes. I decided to just knock on the door and ask "How much do I owe?" put that amount on the counter and leave.

Before I could do that, I was stopped cold by the female voice, because this time I recognized who it was. "I invoke our spirit guardian to show us the way," Leslie Waters Sumac said with great authority. Somehow I couldn't imagine the Dolly Parton look-alike and owner of the Prince and Pauper invoking spirits, but she was clearly doing that. People had stopped shouting and were so quiet I couldn't hear a thing, even though I had cupped my hands against the door to improve my chances of hearing every word.

A low, undecipherable chant started and continued. I decided it was time for me to leave. In my mind, the voices of Ed and Harvey both said, "We told you so." I turned and fled down the stairs. As I pulled open the curtain, Steven Roberts opened the shop door and walked in. We looked at each other in startled amazement. Regaining his composure first, he said, "Lucy forgot to lock the door again, I see. I'll bet you came in to buy those nice sandals you have on, didn't you?"

His voice was friendly but the stony stare he gave me told a different story. I'd seen that look before in men's eyes, and it wasn't good. His large body blocked my only exit.

"Yes, but no one is here to take my money. I'll just take these off and return tomorrow to pay for them. Will you let Lucy know that when you see her?" I watched his tense body movement and his cold eyes while he closed the door.

I continued to talk and his emotions seemed to ratchet down and he spoke in a friendlier manner. "So you haven't seen her at all? I thought I saw you come from behind the curtain," he said, and he smiled. I couldn't help but notice what big teeth he had, wolf-like, in fact.

"I'd just stepped into the back when I heard you open the door. No one is home, it seems," I replied, trying hard to act innocent.

I reached down and took off the sandals, grabbed my shoes, put them on and picked up my bag. "Jazz is outside waiting for me. Good to see you again, Mr. Roberts."

"Please, call me Steven. And I'll tell Lucy you want the sandals," he informed me.

The bell tinkled again on my way out. "Jazz, let's get out of Dodge," I said as he dutifully trotted beside me down the narrow street. My nerves were bothered by the encounter. The short walk through the village helped me to decide nothing sinister could possibly happen in such a beautiful place. On the other hand, I'd been a police detective for so long that being suspicious and watchful had become a way of life for me. It didn't take ten minutes to get back to Maple Cottage and I sent Jazz home to Rodney.

The front door lock was difficult to open, which it hadn't been before. I put my bag down so I could work with it. I'd have to ask Rodney if he could get it repaired. I definitely wanted a solid, working lock on the door. Having no luck after a few minutes I decided to go around back and go in through the kitchen door. There was a smaller key for that one. Walking around the house I noticed an ivy-covered shed I hadn't seen before behind the cottage. The kitchen door opened easily and I went to the front door, opened it from the inside and brought in my string bag. I played with the lock a while longer but still couldn't fix it. I walked over to the phone and dialed Rodney's number. He didn't answer so I left a message asking that he have the lock repaired as soon as possible.

As soon as I put the phone down, it rang. I picked it up, knowing it was Ed. I couldn't wait to tell him about my day's activities and of my suspicions. I must be imagining wrongdoing where none existed. Ed always made a point of bursting whatever bubble I had turned into blimp size.

"Ed, I'm so glad you called," I said before I heard the voice.

"Honey, it's not Ed. It's your husband. How the hell are you? I'm here in England, come all the way from Tacoma, Washington, to be with my bride."

"Dan? What are you doing in England? If you recall, we divorced years ago when you left me for your secretary. By the way, how are Connie and the twins? Are they with you?"

"Connie and I have had a, shall we say, falling out. I called Ed and got him to tell me where you are. I don't think he likes me very much, does he? He took a certain tone, if you know what I mean."

"He likes you better than I do. The last time you called, when I was still in Las Vegas, I hung up on you. Didn't that give you a hint, Dan, that I want nothing more to do with you?"

"Ah, you know you don't mean that. It's just like that song says, 'The first cut is the deepest.' You and I, we cut each other up pretty good."

"Why are you here, Dan? This is the last thing I'm going to say to you before I hang up."

"Calm down. Jeez, I can't believe you lasted as a cop. You fly off the handle way too fast. I'm here because I want us to get back together. It was wrong of me to leave you for Connie like I did, but she was pregnant. What was an honest, self-respecting man like me supposed to do in such a situation?"

That comment was so stupid I couldn't come up with a reply fast enough. It gave him time to top himself. What did I ever see in this total jerk? I shook my head in wonder over my lack of taste in men. Of course, all my friends, especially Harvey and Ed, had told me that often.

"If you want to know the truth I heard you'd come into some money from that partner of yours that was murdered down in Vegas. I always thought the two of you would get hooked up, if you know what I mean. Anyway, I heard he left you a bundle."

"Dan, this is the first time in years I've heard you tell me the truth. So you want to be with me because I have money now, is that it?"

"Yes, but in a good way. You and I were so hot together. Do you remember the night in the back of my '88 Cadillac? I knew I loved big back seats for a reason."

I blushed at the memory then got mad. I hung up the phone. How, I wondered, do I get a restraining order against Dan in England?

Chapter Eight

I kept my hand on the phone for a moment. Every time I heard my ex-husband's voice it unnerved me. And what in the world was he doing in England? Did he really think I'd have anything to do with him? Of course, I knew what he wanted because he'd told me. Money.

A cup of coffee would help me settle down so I headed toward the kitchen. I rattled around the tiny area, put together a pot of coffee and sat down at the table to wait for it to brew. Except for the fact it was haunted, I liked this cottage. Sun streamed in through the windows and flowers peeked around the outside sill.

I got up and walked over to the door, opened it, and went into the backyard. Birds twittered in the branches of the rowan trees that stood at the back of the house. Rodney's gardeners kept the grounds immaculate. It wasn't as large as my yard in Las Vegas, but it was certainly more beautiful. I sat down on a weathered wicker chair and breathed in the air. It smelled of freshly mowed grass, flowers and trees. The sky couldn't have been a finer shade of blue. What had I been thinking, that I wanted to go back to that high desert heat?

The coffee maker beeped at me, letting me know it was ready. I hurried back into the cottage and got the largest cup from the cupboard. The coffee smelled good as I poured it to the top of the pink stoneware mug.

I went out to the yard to settle into a comfortable chair and drink my coffee. I took a sip, then rested my head against the curved back and let the sun warm my face. After a few more sips of coffee I set the cup down on the matching wicker table. I could tell there might be a nap in my future. My eyes felt heavy and I slumped down into the cushions and stretched my legs out, toes wiggling, in the cool green grass.

VVRROOMM. I opened my eyes and sat straight up. The gentle afternoon quiet had shattered and the deafening noise didn't go away. It got louder and was coming from the front of the cottage. I knew what it sounded like but I was in a small English village, not Las Vegas.

I walked around the side of the house and looked into the front yard. There, in all its noisy glory was a Harley-Davidson. A black-leather-clad figure straddled the bike. The helmet looked like something out of a space movie. I cautiously moved toward the motorcycle and the rider.

After some unsnapping and grappling, he removed his helmet and there stood my ex-husband, Dan.

He gave me a big smile. "Eva May, it's been too long. You look like hell but it's good to see you anyway."

"I can't say the same. You look like always, Dan, and I'm not glad to see you. Go away." I had all intentions of going back to my nap in the backyard. I wanted nothing to do with this man.

"Ah, come on. I know you're mad at me but I came all this way to take you on a picnic. I have everything ready for us. Where's a good place for us to go, someplace quiet and romantic." He grinned and it made his eyes crinkle. "You can tell me what a louse I am and I'll agree. I wasn't very nice to you, Eva May."

"Go away. I want nothing to do with you," I repeated but I could tell my tone of voice had changed. I wondered what it was about this man that pulled me in every time. He was a liar, cheat and thief. My kind of guy!

I looked the machine over and ran my hand along the fender. "Where did you find a Harley? Don't you know it's quiet and peaceful here? This is not the place to be roaring around on one of these." I knew why Dan had done it. He understood my love for all things motorcycle. One of my longest-lasting bad relationships had been with a motorcycle cop in Las Vegas. Ernie had been a dancer in one of the shows but made a career move over to the police department. I always thought it was because he knew how great he looked in the uniform and on the bike.

"You know me, May. I can pull the rabbit out of the hat. Speaking of which, your riding gear and helmet are in the left saddlebag. Can I come in while you change? I need to make a pit stop." He slung his long legs over the bike and started moving toward the front door.

"It's to the right, next to the kitchen," I called to his retreating back. I walked around the Harley and looked at it closely. It was a black-and-chrome Electra Glide, large, loud and lovely.I opened the saddlebag, more like a small suitcase, and pulled out a leather jacket, boots, gloves and helmet, all in my size. I looked into the other bag and found a couple of plastic dishes that held some sort of delicious-smelling food. Dan had been a busy boy, no doubt.

I gathered up the black leather jacket and boots, but left the helmet and gloves for when I came out, dressed and ready to rumble.

I went into the cottage and directly into my bedroom, where I quickly stripped down to my bra and panties.

"You still have that beautiful body." Dan lounged against the door, which I had left open.

My heart pounded and I felt a rush of desire whenever I came within a mile of this man. "I thought you said I looked like hell." I couldn't stop my eyes from looking up and down his tall frame.

Dan moved into the room and started taking off his leathers. I walked over to him, put my arms around his neck and pulled his face down to mine, a considerable distance since he is tall. Our lips met and he lifted me up and held me against him. "I hate you," I moaned in between kisses. He carried me over to the bed and put me down gently.

"I knew this would happen," he said, an evil glint in his eyes.

"Me, too," I agreed, as I reached for him.

* * *

"I'm starving. When did you last eat anything?" Dan felt my ribs.

"It's been awhile. Don't recall what I last ate. How about that food you brought with you?" I played with his curly hair, which had turned gray. "You need to get a dye job."

"Connie told me that, too."

I moved slightly away from him and rose up on my elbow. "You just brought me crashing back to earth with that comment, Bozo. What are you doing? Better yet, what am I doing?" I moved to get out of bed but he pulled me back.

"Don't take it that way. You and I were made for each other. We both know that. I'd never have left you. If you remember, you're the one who walked out on me."

"You got your secretary pregnant. What would you expect me to do?" My anger increased. It was just like always; nothing had changed.

"Yes, I did. And I came to you and told you about it. Then, if you remember, I got down on my knees and begged you to forgive me. The next thing I know, you'd quit your job and moved to Las Vegas. Even that crazy friend of yours agreed you ran away. Why did you do that, honey? I never would have left you for Connie. I would have supported the twins, of course, but I never would have married her if you hadn't left me high and dry."

I wanted to bash his head in. "So this is entirely my fault. I'm glad you explained it to me. Here I thought you'd cheated on me and now I find out I'm to blame for the breakup of our marriage." I got out of bed and started pulling on clothes, ready to throw the first thing I could get my hands on that would be heavy enough to hurt him. "I told you I hated you and I do. Get out of here. I never want to see your face again." My hands were on my hips, my belligerent stance, and I knew it was a very good thing I didn't have my gun handy.

"Listen, it's good we're talking about this. But keep it down, will you? You don't want your roommate hearing this conversation."

My entire body chilled. "What roommate?" I asked, not wanting to know the answer.

"The young blonde woman. When I washed my hands in the bathroom she was there. I could have sworn I'd closed the door but I saw her face in the mirror and then when I turned around she'd disappeared. She looked so sad. Have you two had a fight or something?"

I sat down on the edge of the bed. The village tale that only women could see her must be wrong. "Her name is Sarah and she's the ghost that haunts this cottage."

Dan's eyes got wide. "No way!"

"Yep, it's true. I thought I'd imagined it but now there are two of us who've seen her. Dan, I think she was murdered and something is still going on in this village about her."

"Don't go pulling me into one of your crime scenes. You need to get out of this place. Pack up and we'll go find a B&B somewhere. I passed a hundred of them on the way here."

"I can't just run away, Dan." I looked up at him and I could tell he wanted to say something.

Finally he got the words out. "Why not? That's your specialty." His words were laser cold and true.

For once, Dan left me speechless. But he made a good point. Packing up and leaving seemed like a wonderful idea to me, too. "Let me throw some clothes together and let's get out of here," I said, scared and ready to run.

* * *

"Dan, stop licking my toes," I mumbled. "It tickles." I reached down and swatted at him but he kept it up. I opened one eye and watched Jazz continue to lick my toes while Rodney looked on from his wheelchair. "Sorry to wake you, but the locksmith is here to repair the door."

"Isn't there a Harley in front of the cottage?" I asked as I rubbed my eyes.

"No, but there's a very noisy old diesel lorry that belongs to Mr. Vaughn, the locksmith."

I leaned forward in the lawn chair and pulled my feet toward me. "That's enough toe cleaning for one day, Jazz." I petted his soft fur, warm from the sun, and stood up. "My nap lasted longer than I'd planned and the dream I had was so realistic," I said to Rodney, who had backed his chair up a little ways so I had more room.

"Was it pleasant?" he asked, as he looked up at me.

"It was about Dan, my ex-husband, who'd called just before I went to sleep. The thing is, he looked like a cross between Richard Gere and Benecio Del Toro. In reality, he's a short little guy with a potbelly. Dan's personality was the same, though, rotten through and through. Can I get a restraining order against him in England, Rodney?"

"I don't know, but you can ask my solicitor tonight. That is if you can join us. I'm having a little to-do about eightish. Nothing dressed up, you understand. Come as you are and that would be delightful."

I looked down at my ratty jeans and said, "Oh, no; I'll come but I'll wear something else."

Rodney smiled. "Let's go around front and see how Mr. Vaughn is doing with the broken lock. I can't imagine how that happened."

Chapter Nine

Mrs. Long opened the door when I arrived a little after eight. I had taken longer than usual to get dressed and I felt nervous but compelled to be there. Sarah cropped up in my mind often and now in my dreams. She had taken hold and wasn't letting go.

I had never been inside Rodney's house and my mouth fell open when I walked into the foyer. It was huge and reminded me of museums I'd been to in the States. Curved stairways on each side of the entryway led to the upper floors. Ancestral portraits marched up both sides of the stairway walls and an enormous crystal chandelier hung from the top of a rotunda ceiling. Cold marble floor stretched in all directions. Suits of armor stood sentinel at several entryways. I expected Dracula to walk through one of the closed doors that ringed the room. Even knowing Rodney as little as I did, I knew this house did not fit his nature.

"It's quite something, isn't it?" Mrs. Long asked politely. "I've worked here over forty years and it still takes my breath away. It's most beautiful during the holidays. We have crowds who come up then. The whole village is here plus Mr. Rodney's friends from his work at university." She looked at the dark, tapestry-covered walls with obvious affection.

"Yes, I must admit I've never seen anything like it," I said. "Do most of the manor homes in England resemble this?"

"Unfortunately, no. For most families it's too much upkeep. We're lucky, though. Our little village has been able to survive quite nicely as has this estate. Let me show you where the group has gathered, Miss Scott. This way, please."

I followed her ample body through the foyer to a door that didn't

63

have a suit of armor guarding it. The little haunted cottage I occupied was beginning to appeal to me even more after seeing this house. Before we'd gone too far, I noticed a side table with framed photographs on it. "Is this Rodney's family?"

Mrs. Long turned back toward me and looked at the photos. She picked one up and said, "This is Lady Violet, his mother, and his father, Lord Willsdon. I've been in service for the family my entire adult life," she said with pride in her voice.

"Lady Violet looks very young," I commented. She was a beautiful creature, frail and fair. "Her husband looks old enough to be her grandfather."

"She adored Master Rodney. He was such a handsome baby. She came alive when he was born. Of course, in those days, it wasn't all that unusual for a young girl to be married to a much older man. It's the way some of these manor houses have survived, by combining family fortunes. Old Lord Willsdon loved Lady Violet more than anything or anybody on earth." She sighed and put the photo back on the table. "I miss those days. It's not the same now."

I continued to look at the photos. "Who is this woman? She looks familiar."

Mrs. Long looked at the picture and said, "That's Mrs. Angelina Waters, our village 'practitioner of the arts,' during her lifetime. She's also the mother of Leslie Waters Sumac, owner of the Prince & Pauper Pub. Have you met her yet?"

Now that she'd told me who the woman was, I could see the remarkable resemblance. "I have met Leslie and she looks like a carbon copy of her mother, doesn't she?"

Mrs. Long smiled and nodded. "Yes, she's just like her mother, in many ways. Leslie is our tie to the old ways now, just as her mother was before."

"The 'old ways' seems to come up in many conversations," I commented. "Where is a photo of Rodney when he was young?"

She looked over the large collection and selected one that was hidden in the back. "Here he is as a teenager, before he lost his legs in Northern Ireland." She handed it to me.

He was with a group of young men and all of them looked carefree and happy. They stood in front of a red sports car. "He doesn't resemble his parents at all, does he?" I commented.

She took the photo out of my hands and said, "You should really join the group now, Miss Scott." Carefully, she placed the picture in the back, hidden from view.

Mrs. Long led me further down the hall to a set of double doors, opened them and said, "Lord Willsdon, your special guest has arrived." The small group of people drinks in hand, turned to look at me. As soon as I entered the room, I heard the doors close behind me. A large fireplace with an intricately carved mantle took up a portion of the wall I faced. Comfortable chairs and two beautifully covered pale yellow silk couches looked inviting.

"Eva May, I'm so glad you found the time to join us." Rodney rolled toward me, Jazz followed close behind. "Miss Scott, May to all of us here, is the best tenant I've ever had in the cottage, but she keeps breaking locks." Everyone smiled graciously.

I didn't break the lock, but someone had. Rodney had already left when the lock repairman told me it had been tampered with. This didn't seem to be the right moment to mention it, though.

"I'm pleased that you invited me, Lord Willsdon." I used the name as Mrs. Long had, but it felt awkward. I followed him and took a seat in a dark leather chair. I looked around and realized several of the guests were familiar to me. Jazz came up to me, wagging his tail, and I ruffled his ears and put my nose on his nose. "Are you the best dog in the world?" He wiggled his agreement then returned to Rodney's side.

"Please, call me Rodney as you've been doing. Lord Willsdon was my father and I never use the title. Mrs. Long is the only one who calls me that. Have you met my solicitor, Michael Reed?"

Light brown hair fell over the forehead of the man Rodney had introduced. He looked too young to be an attorney. "No, I haven't but it's a pleasure to meet you," I said.

"I believe May is going to have some legal questions to ask you, Michael. It seems her ex-husband is a nasty lot and won't leave her alone. He's even followed her to England."

"My, that's too bad. We can talk later. Be glad to help," he said in a flat, monotone voice.

"Thank you, Mr. Reed."

"Michael will do. We're quite informal around here, unlike some parts of the country. Think it has to do with the way we're so insular. Not too many new people move in or out around here. It's quite incestuous, now that I think about it." I couldn't imagine this man swaying a jury. His voice almost put me to sleep.

"Oh, you do go on so, Michael," Leslie Waters Sumac, owner of the pub, answered. She wasn't showing as much cleavage as the day I'd met her, but her dress was a shocking shade of Kelly green and was so tight I wondered how she could breath. She sat with her shapely legs and small feet curled under her on the yellow couch. Her stilettos, also bright green, lay on the floor. She looked very much at home and exactly like her mother in the photo I'd just seen.

"And this enticing lady," Rodney said, "is Lucinda – known as Lucy – Davis, who owns the shoe shop in the village."

"I've been in your shop but didn't get to meet you. I need to come in and pay you for the sandals I tried on and want to buy," I said to Lucy, who sat sedately on the other end of the couch from Leslie. Her suit was dark, very conservative, and her dour expression made her look as though she might be attending a funeral. I wondered if she had a headache because her salt-and-pepper colored hair was pulled so tightly away from her face. I was sure there was a neat bun at the nape of her neck. I'd have to check as soon as I could see back there.

"Yes, Steven told me of your visit. My pleasure to meet you." She nodded her head in my direction. "I've got the shoes you selected put away."

"Thank you. I'll try to come in tomorrow and pick them up," I answered.

Rodney continued the introductions, but I had already met Joan Pritchard, librarian.

"Nice to see you again," I commented.

"Yes, indeed. Do stop in and we'll chat more about your ghost, my cousin Sarah." Her smile looked genuine. The summer dress she wore was a pretty pastel pink and it made her look young. Her brown hair just touched her shoulders and was cut in a youthful bob. Unfortunately, her hands gave away her age. They were mottled with brown spots and the veins stood out in ridges.

The last person to be introduced was Steven Roberts, owner of the grocery and the man who'd barred my exit from Lucy's shoe shop. At least that's how it had seemed to me. He sat in an armless, green velvet brocade-covered chair next to Rodney. Seeing the two men together made me realize how frail Rodney looked. Steven had not missed many meals over the years. Even though he was tall, his body was soft and paunchy-looking.

"So, do tell us, May, why do you keep breaking Rodney's door locks?" Leslie asked, her blonde hair shining like a golden cap.

"I just know that when I came home from the village, the front door wouldn't open. I went in through the kitchen door. The locksmith told me it had been tampered with. Oh, and by the way, I saw an ivy-covered shed behind the cottage. What is it used for, Rodney?"

I noticed that Leslie and Steven looked at each other as soon as I mentioned the dilapidated building.

"It was a gardening shed, I believe," Rodney replied. "I've never seen it used though, at least not in my lifetime. I know my mother warned me about going near it – said there were wasps' nests around the eaves. I can't believe your lock was tampered with. I'll call Mr. Vaughn and speak to him about it tomorrow."

"Thanks, Rodney, he got it fixed so the lock is working again. Do you think Mrs. Long would know the answer about the shed?" I asked. "She's been here longer than any of you, hasn't she?" This time Lucy and Joan looked at each other. "It just struck me as odd having grounds and buildings that are so perfectly manicured and then here's this unkempt little building."

"Well, yes, I suppose so," Leslie answered. "When are you coming back to my pub for some spotted dick?" she asked.

I smiled. She'd changed the subject. There must be something about the shed they didn't want me to know. "Can't wait for that spotted dick," I replied.

"My, my, you naughty girls. I'm going to ring Mrs. Long and get her in here to refresh our drinks before you two go over the entire pub menu. May, we must get you something to drink." Rodney rolled his chair over to the mantle and pulled a black cord that was next to it.

I didn't hear a thing but Mrs. Long was in the room in about one second. She must have been waiting just outside the door to react as quickly as she did.

Rodney turned his chair toward her and asked for the drink cart to be brought in, and I watched with interest.

In a few moments, she returned with a cart that resembled the ones flight attendants used on airlines to provide drinks and snacks to the passengers. "Surely it's not what I think it is."

"If you think it's used on airlines, you're correct. I'm testing it out for the university. They have a contract to provide a more streamlined version. I've had it now for about a month."

"I never would have come up with that explanation. I thought maybe you'd attended a hangar sale for airline paraphernalia."

Everyone laughed. "I'm afraid it's not that interesting," he replied. "It does seem to be better than the older version, don't you agree, Mrs. Long?"

"Yes, sir, most definitely. Much lighter to maneuver and easier to use."

"So that leads me to believe you tried the previous version before you got this one." I got up and walked over to the cart and looked at it. To my inexperienced eyes it was like what I'd seen on airlines for years.

"Oh, yes, we must do that sort of thing so we have something to compare," he said.

"I'm baffled by the reason that a military-based university such as yours would be testing airline carts." I leaned down and looked at the sides, hoping to find some revelation that would make it clear. It looked like any other cart I'd seen.

"Okay, I give up. What's the big deal?"

"I do love your American slang. The 'big deal' is that this cart contains a handgun that can be used in case of terrorists on a flight."

"No way," I said, in my slangy way. "Show me!"

Rodney looked around at the others in the group. Most of them were grinning. "Do you mind seeing this demonstration once more for our American visitor?" he asked.

"Of course not," Leslie said. "But if you don't mind, I'll go visit the facilities during this part of the show." She put on her shockingly green spike heels, stood up and moved toward the open doors.

"I think I'll go, too," Lucy and Joan said in unison.

"You must have some large bathroom, Rodney," I said as I watched the retreating backs of the women.

"I don't blame them. They always do that when it gets dull,"

Michael, the boring attorney, said.

"How many times have we seen this demonstration?" Steven asked. "I'm off to join the girls, who aren't really in the loo but having smokes on the terrace." He got up and left the room through the door Mrs. Long had used to bring in the cart.

"But this is fascinating," I said, already pulling on knobs and opening cubbyholes on the cart. I could tell that Mrs. Long wanted to smack my hands for being so nosy, but I kept it up. Until Rodney told me to stop playing, I was going to find out where the gun was located.

He watched with a bemused look on his face. "This is excellent, actually. We need another person to see if they can crack the code. So far, no one has."

I kept up my search. "If this is supposed to be so secretive, why do all of these people know about it?"

"I've been using this group as my guinea pigs for years. I trust all of them."

"But you don't know me, so why am I going to get the demonstration?"

"You're a detective. I know all about you, May. Surely you must realize that I check out my renters very closely. I can't just have any Tom, Dick, or Jane using the cottage."

I pulled out each drawer and looked underneath it. "I've put in my retirement papers. But then you know that, don't you?"

"Yes, I do. In fact, May, I have a little secret to confess." Rodney rolled closer to me.

"I thought you said you'd told her already," Michael said. "How very annoying that you haven't done that, Rodney."

"I meant to get around to it, but then there was the lock problem and I got sidetracked. Michael and I have a mystery to solve and we need your help."

Chapter Ten

"What sort of a mystery?" I asked, going back to my chair.

"First, would you like a drink, May?" Rodney said.

I turned to Mrs.Long and asked if she had coffee. "No, ma'am, but I can certainly make a pot."

Before I could object that it would be too much trouble, she had bustled from the room. "What mystery?" I asked again.

"We believe there is some sort of blackmail going on in the village. I've had some strange telephone calls and Michael has received a threatening letter."

"About what?" This trip was getting more interesting by the minute.

Michael looked at Rodney before he started to speak. "I know this sounds bizarre, but it's something to do with 'the old ones'."

"I don't follow. And why do you think I can help?"

"You're a tourist. Everyone in the village knows that. You could, for lack of a better term, do some 'snooping' for us," Rodney said as he petted Jazz.

"So I'd be sort of a private detective. What did the letter say, Michael?"

"It made reference to the ancestors of this estate and that 'the old ones' made it possible for Rodney to live here. That 'nothing was as it seemed.' I've gone over every conceivable item concerning this property and everything is in order. We can't make any sense of it."

"And the phone calls, Rodney?" I shifted in the chair so I could watch him as he spoke. Body language was a tool and I'd used most of my life, even before I went into police work. A friend back in Tacoma, Washington, had told me it was my innate psychic ability, which always made me laugh because I didn't believe a word of it.

"The caller, and I couldn't tell if it was a man or woman, told me that I was in danger because the village needed an heir for this estate and I couldn't give it to them. Therefore, the caller wanted me to sign the property over to my American relative, who is married and has several children. It was my 'duty' to do this so the linage will continue."

"And what does the American heir have to say on the subject?"

"Good grief. You don't think I've told that oaf? I met him only once, when we were on holiday in the States. I can't imagine anything worse than he and his horrible brood moving in here with me." It didn't take psychic ability to see that Rodney was upset. His face was red and he clenched the arms of the wheelchair. Jazz got up and put his head on his master's lap. Rodney calmed as he petted his beloved dog. "Please forgive the outburst, but this is a subject that just won't go away. In fact, I had a call this afternoon, soon after I returned from the cottage. It's as if they know my comings and goings so they always call when I'm at home."

Mrs. Long entered the room with a coffee tray. "I do hope I'm not intruding," she said as she sat the tray on a table next to my chair.

"I'd say you have perfect timing, Mrs. Long." I responded, reaching for the rose-covered china pot.

Jazz walked over to me, his plumy white tail moving in hopes of getting a treat. "There's nothing here that would interest you." I ruffled his ears and scratched under his chin.

Mrs. Long exited the room, closing the door behind her.

"Michael and I have discussed the situation extensively and think you are the one to help sort it out. That is, if you'd be willing to give up some of your holiday. And of course, there will be remuneration."

"I can't 'pretend' to be a PI while I'm still an employee of the Las Vegas Metro Police Department so payment isn't necessary. I don't see why a little snooping wouldn't be allowed, though. Truth is, I do it anyway. It's my nature." I poured a cup of coffee into the delicate cup and took a sip. It was the worst coffee I'd ever had in my life. It tasted like dirty hot water. Trying not to make too much of it, I put the cup onto the tray and settled back in my chair. "I think I can help you."

"Good form. What do we do next? Should we give you the letter to look at? Have the telephone tapped?" Rodney asked. Jazz had given up on treats and plopped down next to the wheelchair.

"Yes, I'd like to see the letter. As for a phone tap, your local police can take care of that. In fact, that's whom you should task with this. I could work with them, if they wanted."

Michael shifted in his chair and shook his head. "That's the point. We don't want anyone knowing about this."

I looked at both Rodney and Michael. "People know anyway. The ones who are threatening you expect you not to go to law enforcement. That's exactly why you need to bring them into this now. Your point that I'm a foreigner goes both ways. I don't know English law or how it operates so I'd be fumbling around causing more trouble than I'm worth. I know you don't want to hear this, but you need to contact your constable. Blackmail situations can get deadly fast."

"I had hopes you could fix everything and no one would be the wiser. This is more complicated than I'd thought, but dangerous? You think it could come to that?" Rodney asked, concern showing on his face.

"Aren't you making too much of it, May?" Michael said.

"I don't think so. Blackmail situations are premeditated. It's like a spider web has been spun and you can't tell from which direction the danger is going to come. The caller threatened you, Rodney. If I were you, I'd call the police right now. If you'd like, I'll do it for you."

Both double doors opened and the other guests entered. Leslie asked, "Blimey, it looks gloomy in here. Does that mean May couldn't figure out the bells and whistles on the airline cart?"

Steven, Lucy, and Joan stood a little behind Leslie. Mrs. Long chose that moment to come into the room and asked if we needed anything else. She stood next to Leslie.

"I had no luck, that's true," I said to Leslie. "Rodney, do you want me to take care of that situation we discussed? I could start the process from the cottage, if you'd like." I looked at Rodney and Michael, hoping I'd get permission to call the police.

"Yes, let's go that route. Don't you agree, Michael?"

"I'd wait, but it's your call, Rodney, not mine."

"What on earth are you being so mysterious about?" Leslie asked, as she moved toward the couch and sat down. The others followed, except for Mrs. Long, who still awaited directions from Rodney.

"Nothing mysterious," Rodney said. "That's all for now, Mrs. Long."

I stayed and chatted a few more minutes then told the group I was going to return to the cottage. I rose from the chair, said my goodbyes and headed toward the double doors. Rodney wheeled after me and I opened the door so he could go through. "I can see myself out, you don't have to escort me," I said to him, Jazz following close behind.

"Do you think it's the correct thing to do, calling the police? Michael didn't agree with it." He rolled to a stop in front of the massive front door.

"He was right, though, in saying it's your decision. He works for you, not the other way around. Another thing, don't mention this to anybody else – especially your friends and Mrs. Long."

"You certainly can't think they're involved. I've known them all my life."

"That's just it, Rodney, we don't know who's behind this. Take my advice and keep it quiet. I'll call the police station tonight and will be in touch." I gave Jazz a quick pat on the head, thanked Rodney, opened the door and walked out into the dark night.

The walk back to the cottage was peaceful. The stars were out and an almost-full moon helped lead the way. It occurred to me that I was probably surrounded by ghosts of   locals. If they were like Sarah, though, I wasn't frightened. She was just very sad. I hadn't seen her recently but sensed that her spirit still occupied the little cottage.

The front door opened with no problem and as soon as I turned on a lamp, I headed for the telephone to call. The thin telephone directory had the number for the local police station prominently displayed on the cover.

After two rings, it was answered. I provided the information requested and was told Detective Constable Johnston would contact me within an hour. While I waited I did laundry, and sorted through several kitchen cabinets to see if I needed to walk to the grocery in the morning. I was perched on a chair trying to reach for a pretty lavender teacup overlooked in the back of the cabinet when the shrill ring of the telephone startled me. I scrambled down from the chair and ran into the living room to answer it.

"Hello?"

"Is this Ms. Scott?"

"Yes."

"DC Johnston here. I believe you wanted to talk to me about a possible blackmail scheme?"

"You're the gentleman who helped get me out of that tight parking space in front of the grocery. We meet again," I said.

"Yes, so we do. Now, how can I help you, Ms. Scott?"

Chapter Eleven

DC Johnston had agreed to meet with me, along with Rodney, at Michael's law office in the village. The time was set for 10:00 a.m. and each of us showed up a little early. I had plans to purchase a few items at the grocery afterwards, so came with my cotton carrier tucked into my handbag. It was a relief not to have to deal with Costco–sized portions, but shop on an every other day schedule. I liked it.

It amazed me that I was blasé about my houseguest, Sarah. She had been in my dream last night. Sitting on one of the huge sarsens that ringed the outer circle of Stonehenge, her shoulder-length blonde hair glowed in the evening twilight. The dress she wore emphasized a small waist and slender arms. While I watched, in my dream, Sarah beckoned for me to join her. I did start to move forward but was pulled back to reality by the ringing of the telephone. As I got out of the warm bed, went into the living room and reached for the annoying instrument, I realized that I would rather be with Sarah in the dream than talking with Rodney about setting a meeting time with a police detective and a lawyer.

By the time I'd showered, made coffee and re-checked my grocery list, it was time to leave. Rodney had offered to pick me up in his huge Suburban but I had declined. I enjoyed the short walk along the tree-lined cobblestone sidewalk, which was next to the river. I took a few minutes, stood on the arch-shaped bridge and watched the white swans as they glided under the long-limbed trees whose branches dipped into the water. They reminded me of lines that I had inadvertently let tangle in the water when I had gone trout fishing with my grandfather in the cold Montana streams.

The solicitor's office was above the bank. In order to get to it, you went into the bank and took the stairs to the second floor. I didn't see an elevator but there must have been one somewhere to accommodate the physically handicapped, such as Rodney. I would have to ask him where the secret entrance was located.

I couldn't help but compare the office to those I'd visited many times in Tacoma, Washington, and Las Vegas, Nevada. It more closely resembled one in Tacoma, in that it was furnished with antiques, muted colors and looked elegantly expensive. The Las Vegas version was sleekly modern and bright.

As soon as I entered, an older lady who introduced herself as Mrs. Perkins led me into a small conference room. Rodney sat at the round oak table in his wheelchair. "Come sit next to me," he said, and I did. The heavy chair was hard to pull away from the table but comfortable once I got situated. Almost as soon as I sat down, Michael walked into the room.

"I'm going to guess that both you and Michael know Detective Constable Johnston." I said.

"Never made his acquaintance, I'm afraid," Rodney replied.

"Neither have I," chimed in Michael.

"I thought everybody knew and /or is related to everybody else in this village. Don't tell me you let someone slip in who's actually new," I kidded. "I met him outside the grocery and he helped me with a parking problem."

"We are, as I've said, an incestuous lot," Michel replied. "I'll have to check on how this new man came on board. He's probably related to someone in the village. Any wagers on that?"

I was about to respond that I'd take the bet when he was ushered into the room. My favorite television shows have been *Midsomer Murders* and the "Inspector Lynley" series on the BBC. This was my first encounter with an English detective on the job and I was intrigued.

He reached out his hand to me and said, "Pleasure to meet you again, Ms. Scott. I'm Detective Constable Johnston." I briefly shook his hand and he repeated the process with Rodney and Michael. He took a seat on the other side of Rodney and asked that Michael join us at the table. The detective was firmly in charge.

"You two know each other, then?" Michael asked.

I looked at DC Johnston and said, "I told them we'd met."

"It was a case of too many vehicles for the limited amount of space," he answered. "I would have preferred that we do this meeting at the Station but I could understand Ms. Scott's request that we meet here. It will give us more privacy. Lord Willsdon, please start." DC Johnston had his moleskine notebook out, pen poised at the ready.

While Rodney and Michael gave him the information they'd relayed to me the previous evening, I observed DC Johnston. He was probably in his early forties, tall, with a clean-shaven face. His thick brown hair was cut short and the suit he wore was lightweight wool, a dark grayish-blue mixture. The shirt was crisply white and the tie was probably a regimental or university stripe but I didn't know enough about that to identify it correctly. His face seemed serious as he talked with the men and he occasionally glanced my way to see if I was following or had anything to offer. I barely shook my head to indicate I had nothing to add. He nodded imperceptibly and I doubted if either Rodney or Michael caught it. So far he got all A's in my book.

"Could I please have the letter that you received, Mr. Reed?"

"Of course, I have it here in this folder, plus the envelope it came in." He handed it over to the detective.

"Does anyone else in the office open your mail and read it?"

"No, it's just left for me in a small cubicle that's in the main office area. Mrs. Perkins sorts it each day. Each of the attorneys's have their own box.

"So, in actuality, anyone has access to your mail." He put down his pen, pulled out a pair of plastic gloves from his jacket pocket, which he put on, and opened the folder. "There's no return address nor postage on the envelope. Did you notice that, Mr. Reed?"

"You know, I didn't notice that. I went right to the letter and read it over many times, and then went over the estate papers as well, looking for some sort of clue as to what this is all about."

"I find it interesting that the letter was sent directly to you and not to Lord Willsdon. Why do you think that is, Mr. Reed?" The detective turned slightly to face the attorney.

Michael looked puzzled. "I really can't say. It never crossed my mind to look at it that way. I just saw that my client needed my help and dived in to do that."

"Why didn't you call the police, Mr. Reed? You recognized that it was blackmail, so you'd think the logical thing to do would be to give us a call. Instead, an American tourist who's renting a cottage from Lord Willsdon calls us. Doesn't that strike you as odd, Mr. Reed?"

Michael looked at Lord Willsdon, then to me for support. "I went to my client. It would be his option to bring in the police."

"Did you advise that he do that, Mr. Reed?"

"Well, yes and no. Rodney – Lord Willsdon – and I discussed it at length and decided it would be more appropriate to keep it as quiet as possible. That's why we sought the services of Ms. Scott, since she's an American detective."

Rodney said, "It was my decision not to call you in, I'm afraid. Michael did tell me it would be the best option, but I didn't follow his advice."

"And why do you want to keep this quiet, Lord Willsdon?"

"I want it all to go away. I thought Ms. Scott would be a good choice to find out who was behind this and what they wanted."

DC Johnston looked at the short letter. "It's plain what they want, Lord Willsdon. They want your inheritance. When was the last time you've heard from them?"

"Yesterday, as I mentioned earlier. It was the same sort of call I've received before. It's as though they know my comings and goings. Would tapping the telephone help?" Rodney asked.

"Possibly. Ms. Scott, what do you make of all this?" He directed his attentions to me.

"I think you should look at Rodney's friends and housekeeper. There's something about that group that hasn't set well with me since I arrived. Leslie Sumac, Mrs. Long, and the owner of the grocery, Steven Roberts, make me especially suspicious."

"What have they done to give you that impression?"

"First off, I have to confess to a little snooping."

Rodney and Michael both looked at me in surprise.

"Please continue," DC Johnston requested.

"I went into the village to look around and saw a pair of sandals that I liked in the window of Lucinda Davis' shoe shop. I walked in but no one was there and called out but there wasn't an answer. Then I heard these voices. So, I did what I shouldn't have – I went through the curtain into the back. The voices were coming from up the stairs, so I climbed them and listened outside a closed door." I glanced around to see how this was going over. DC Johnston was expressionless. Rodney and Michael looked mystified.

"I clearly heard Leslie Sumac say something about 'it was done for our protection and if it wasn't kept going the village would die.' There were other voices but there were too many for me to recognize. Then they did some sort of chant, and Leslie asked 'the spirit guardian' to lead them. It was all very eerie. I decided I'd better get back down the stairs and I did, just in time to run into Steven Roberts who was coming into the shop. The way he looked and spoke made me nervous. He commented that Lucy had forgotten to put the 'closed' sign on her door. That told me he was part of the crowd upstairs, but late to the meeting. I got out of there fast."

"Did you tell anyone about this?" the detective asked.

"No, at that time I thought it was some sort of strange meeting, but didn't go beyond that. You have to realize, I've been here less than two weeks and have seen my first ghost-in fact we live together-been privy to a meeting that could have come straight off the 'Sci-Fi' channel and am within a few miles of Stonehenge. I haven't visited the latest sighting of crop circles I saw advertised in the local paper or Glastonbury, where King Arthur's grave is supposedly located. I'm not sure what's considered normal in this area."

"Is there anything else you'd like to add, Ms. Scott?" the detective asked, looking bemused.

"The lock to the front door of the cottage was tampered with. Someone tried to break in."

Chapter Twelve

DC Johnston agreed to set up surveillance, both at the estate and in the lobby of the solicitor's offices. Tapping of the phone would be a part of the process, which made Rodney sigh with relief. I was glad it was out of my hands and into the capable English ones of DC Johnston.

"Ms. Scott, before you go, could I please have a minute?" he asked, as I was about to leave.

Rodney and Michael had their heads together, still sitting at the conference table. At his request, I joined the detective who was standing next to the small windows that looked out onto the high street. I glanced down and saw that foot traffic had increased since I'd entered the building earlier. Of course, it was close to noon, so many of them might be heading off for their lunch. I could see the square, pinkish-colored stone church tower, where Sarah was buried in the tree-shaded graveyard.

"What do you make of this situation, Ms. Scott? Do you seriously think Lord Willsdon's friends are behind it?"

"I only know what I heard and observed. As I said, that could be due to my misunderstanding of local customs. I'm glad the police are now aware of the situation and can get it resolved."

"Yes, I agree that we should have been brought in immediately, but I can understand Lord Willsdon's reluctance. How much longer will you be with us, Ms. Scott? I would like to urge that you stay until we get to the bottom of this. Is that possible?"

"I've booked the cottage until early September, then I'll return to Las Vegas."

"To retire, I think I heard?"

"Yes, to retire. I plan on building a home in the Pahrump area, which is sixty miles west of the city."

"In the wild, cowboy desert?" he asked, as he looked back at Rodney and Michael, who were still talking.

"Yep. But the 'wildest' things these days around Pahrump are the brothels. They're still legal in that part of Nevada."

"I say, how amazing. I must come visit."

"An excellent idea. You'd enjoy yourself, I'm sure. I have some shopping to do, so if you don't mind, I'll be on my way."

"You'll be kept in the loop, Ms. Scott. And if you do decide to leave the area, let me know before you depart."

"No problem with that. And please, call me May." I said a quick goodbye to Rodney and Michael then left the way I had come.

I had a good feeling about the meeting as I walked down the high street. The sun was warm on my face and I enjoyed the bustle of the sidewalk crowd. From the looks of it, there were many tourists visiting this pretty Wiltshire community.

The grocery was busy. I took a hand basket from the stack that was next to the double doors and headed for the peanut butter. Before I got there, I saw Steven Roberts heading my way.

"That was a pleasant get-together at Lord Willsdon's, wasn't it?" he inquired.

His eyes looked shifty to me and I didn't like the way he looked up and down my body. I couldn't imagine why Sarah had found anything about this man attractive. Maybe if I'd met him when he was young it would make sense; but not this brutish thug with the Santa belly and Big Bad Wolf teeth.

"Very enjoyable. It was nice of Rodney – Lord Willsdon – to do that. If you'll excuse me, please…," I murmured as I tried to flee to the safety of the condiments aisle.

"Of course. Good to see you again, May. I say, would you like to go with me to the cinema some evening?" he asked.

This day had taken a definite downturn. "Maybe another time," I said, meaning never.

"Great! I'll call you later this week and we can set a date." He looked like the old fat cat that just ate the canary. "I'll leave you to your shopping now," he said and finally left.

I would quickly unplug the telephone when I returned to the cottage then give everyone I wanted to have it my cell phone number. Come to think of it, that would take care of that rat ex-husband of mine who was lurking around somewhere. I hoped he'd given up and gone away, because I hadn't heard from him since that one call.

Hurriedly I gathered the few items I needed because I didn't want to run into Steven again. The queue for the checkout was slow. After I made it through the line, I was glad to get back to the sunny afternoon.

Since it was on the way to the cottage, I decided to visit Sarah's grave.

This time I didn't have to look around for where she was. I went right to her. The stone had an angel face carved into it and Sarah's name; dates of birth and death listed underneath. Above the face was the inscription "FOREVER OUR BELOVED DAUGHTER." I hadn't noticed on my first visit, but her dad was buried next to her. Rodney had told me that her mother was still alive. I would have to question him further about it. If she was capable, perhaps she could shed light on why Sarah still haunted the cottage. Of course, it might not be such a good idea to bring that up to a woman who, according to Rodney, went "bonkers" after her daughter died.

The hand I felt on my shoulder made me jump and emit a weak scream.

"Oh, I say, please forgive me. I didn't mean to give you such a start," Steven Roberts said.

As usual he stood too close but if I backed up I'd be standing on top of Sarah. I moved sideways in a crab-like movement then turned toward him. "Are you following me, Mr. Roberts?" I asked, feeling anger tinge my cheeks. Dan always said he could tell that he'd really infuriated me when I started turning red like a boiled lobster.

"No, not at all. I often spend my breaks here. It's quiet and in its way, quite beautiful. Don't you agree?" he asked.

"What makes you come here, besides the beauty, of course?" I asked.

"So much of my own history is tied up in this graveyard." He looked around and walked toward a large, ancient stone that stood near the yellowish rock fence. "This is my grandfather and grandmother. Mum and dad are here," he pointed to the next memorial stone."

"Do you visit Sarah?" I asked.

Steven Roberts looked at me with what I took to be contempt. "Sarah ruined my life," he said. "If I talk to her, it's nothing pleasant."

I moved to the front of Sarah's stone and placed my hand on the cool, rough marble. "I've heard the rumors that you were the father of her baby. Is that true?"

He shook his head in a negative way. "No. I've never been the father of any child. Let me show you the main reason I come here".

He moved to an unmarked site. I walked closer to him, but still kept a distance between us. "I don't see a gravesite," I said as I looked at the flat ground.

Steven squatted down and brushed away some leaves. "Now you can see."

I moved closer and looked down at the marker that had taken on the coloration of the soil that surrounded it. Leaning over I saw the name, the dates of birth and death.

"This the reason I have stayed in this claustrophobic village and why I take my breaks in a cemetery." He moved more leaves off the grave and touched his fingers to his lips, then to the marker. "Time to go back to work. Again, sorry to have disturbed you, May. I meant no harm." He left as silently as he had come.

I went back to the marker and read it again. "Angelina Waters" was written in small, elegant script. He visited the grave of Leslie's mother and obviously still loved her.

For a few moments I stood there in the tree-shaded cemetery and thought about Steven Roberts. He was an interesting and scary blend of meek and menacing.

After a few minutes I made my way back onto the busy street and into the sun, which I was grateful to feel again on my face.

By the time I got back to the cottage, I was starved. As soon as I got the front door opened I headed for the kitchen, pulled fresh bread from my bag of groceries and, using the new jar of peanut butter, made two sandwiches. I got a glass down from the cabinet, grabbed the milk from the refrigerator, poured the big glass full, and proceeded to have a feast. I ate standing over the sink, crumbs falling neatly onto the porcelain.

"I see you're still a gourmand, Eva May," a masculine voice said.

I froze in mid-bite. Turning around, crumbs falling from my chin onto my shirt, I watched in horrid fascination as Dan, my ex-husband grinned at me.

Taking a big swallow of milk, I gulped then asked, "How did you get in here?"

"You didn't lock the door, sweetie."

"Don't call me sweetie. You know I hate that."

"Yeah, I know all the buttons to push, don't I?"

"Tell me, please, this is another bad dream. Are you really standing in my kitchen, in England?"

"You've got it, babe."

I turned back to the sink, put my glass down, and wiped the remaining milk ring and crumbs from my mouth. Reluctantly, I faced him.

"I thought you'd gone away. Why are you doing this, Dan? You know I can't stand you, hate you, never wanted to see you again. Why?" If I thought it would have worked, I would have cried to get rid of him.

"I already told you. Connie and me are kaput. After I arm-wrestled Ed into giving me your number, I decided to take a long shot and just show up. Anyway, I needed to get away from Tacoma for awhile." He walked into the kitchen, pulled out a chair and sat at the table. "Mind if I have a sandwich? It's been a long time since I had what they consider a breakfast. I have to tell you, this English food is for the birds." He pulled out bread, rummaged around in the grocery bag, took out sliced ham and cheese. "Got any mayo and mustard? How about some pickles and potato chips; or, since we're in England, crisps?"

I thought about what I was going to do to Ed once I got back to Las Vegas. I bet, after I finished with him, he'd never give out my number again.

"The chips are in the cabinet to the right of the sink – help yourself. I'll be back in a minute." Needing to escape, I left the kitchen for my cozy bedroom, then closed and locked the door. I sat down on the end of the bed and wondered why this was happening.

"Hey, you okay in there?" Dan yelled through the door.

"Just changing into my jeans," I lied.

I sat there for a few minutes then went back into the kitchen. "Get out of my house." I stood over Dan as he gulped down the sandwich. "I don't want you here. Go away."

"Yeah, I know," he agreed. "I shouldn't be here."

"Then why are you?" I pulled out a chair and sat across from him. "And stop eating all of my food. I just got back from the market and you've eaten most of it already."

"I'll replace it. I was hungry. It's been lonely, Eva May, and I missed you. That's the truth."

"You're after Harvey's money, what he left me in his will after he and his wife were murdered."

"I never turn down money, but then it's not being offered to me, is it?"

"No, I don't plan on giving you anything. You broke my heart, Dan. I really loved you. You cheated, lied, left me with nothing. If it hadn't been for Betty I'm not sure I'd still be here."

"Ah, come on. You're making too much out of it. And Betty is nuts. She's crazy as a bedbug."

"She's a wonderful friend to me. So don't say another word about her, unless it's nice. She's a well-respected psychologist and a talented professor.

"Betty is all that, but she's still goofy. If you treated me half as good as you did her I'd never left you for Connie."

"Oh, please, as soon as I saw Connie I knew what sort of woman she is." I was getting mad and this conversation was going nowhere fast.

"Oh, yeah? Was it the short skirts or the orange hair?" He grinned at me like he was enjoying himself.

"This is ridiculous. We're divorced for a reason. I hate you. Now, get out of my house." I stood up and hoped he would, too.

"There's something else I have to tell you, May." He looked up at me. "Sit down and stop hovering over me."

Dan and I are both short. I'm five foot two inches and he towers above me at, maybe, five foot five. I always thought he had a Napoleon Complex, due to his small stature.

"I'll give you two minutes, then you're out of here." I sat back down in the chair and crossed my arms, waiting for his lies to begin.

Chapter Thirteen

"Okay, I'm sitting. Now, spill the beans."

"I'm dying." He continued to eat but he wouldn't look at me.

"Yes, we all are."

Dan stopped chewing, swallowed and looked me in the eyes. "No, babe, I mean I'm really dying. I'm sick." He took a drink of milk and set the glass down.

"I don't believe you. You're trying to get me to feel sorry for you."

"Yeah, that would be nice, if somebody somewhere felt sorry for me."

"Are you serious?"

"Yep. I have, maybe, a year."

"What are you dying of?"

He paused, wiped his mouth and put his hand on top of mine. "Nothing. I made it up. You are so gullible," he said with a big grin.

I yanked my hand away from his and stood up. "Get out, Dan, now, before I call my new buddy who happens to be a Detective Constable. My other best friend is a solicitor. That's English for 'lawyer,' and I know how you hate those types."

"You're calmer these days. I used to love to get you all riled up. Then, if you remember, we'd have wild sex. Interested?" He wiggled his eyebrows at me.

"No, Dan, not even remotely." I tried not to think about the dream I'd had about him not that long ago. I also tried not to laugh. That was the trouble with this man. As much as I tried, I couldn't bring myself to really hate him. Actually, when I didn't want to kill him, he made me laugh. Just as soon as I got him out of the cottage, I was going to call

Janet in Las Vegas and then Betty in Tacoma. My girl friends could help me sort through this mess.

Dan stood up and headed for the front door. "I'm staying at the bed and breakfast that's near the pub, the Prince and Pauper. Have dinner with me, Eva May. Let's talk about the old times that were good. We had some fun days, you know, before you left me for Vegas."

"You certainly believe in revisionist history, don't you, Dan?" I asked, ready to smack him.

"Meet me for dinner. Do you know where this pub is?"

"Yes, and out of curiosity, have you met the pub owner?"

"No, why?" he asked, his hand on the door handle.

"Her name is Leslie Sumac and trust me when I say this, you two are a perfect match for each other," I said, glad to see his back going out the front door.

Going to the phone, I put my hand on the receiver to pick it up and call Betty. The sharp ring startled me and in the process of answering, I dropped it. I leaned over and grabbed for it but managed to push it under the couch, just out of my reach. Crouching down, I stretched my left arm under the couch, and pushed the receiver a little to the side and closer to me. With the second attempt, I got my fingers around it and, sitting on the floor, answered. DC Johnston was on the other end.

Without preamble he said, "I wanted to let you know that there's been a murder."

* * *

I asked Dan to drive me the short distance into the village. He drove his rented Vauxhall as close as we could get before the police stopped us. It was chaotic in the normally pleasant High Street of the village. "I'm going to make a u-turn and point this bucket of bolts in the direction I want to leave. Otherwise, I'll be trapped here for hours," Dan said.

Once he'd parked, we got out and walked toward the explosion site.

"Please step back from the crime scene," a uniformed officer politely requested

"She's with me," DC Johnston said, as he walked in my direction. "I've been watching for your arrival. Come over here and stand next to Lord Willsdon. He's been asking for you."

"Detective Constable Johnston, this is my ex-husband, Dan Peterman."

The two men nodded at each other. I noticed Dan was looking him up and down so I gave him a gentle nudge with my elbow. "Dan, why don't you go back to your bed and breakfast now? I'll call you later."

"Is that a foot I see lying over there?" he asked

"I'm afraid so," I answered.

"Yeah, good idea, I'm leaving. Call me, Eva May. I don't know why you do this stuff for a living."

I thanked him for the ride and hoped I'd never see him again.

DC Johnston and I walked toward a knot of people and Rodney sat in the center in his wheelchair, his hands covered his eyes. I stood next to him and put a hand tentatively on his shoulder. "Rodney, I'm here."

He looked up and his eyes were tortured. "I haven't seen anything like this since Northern Ireland," he said. "Sorry, May, to drag you into this but I thought you could help me."

I asked DC Johnston, who was standing next to me, if I could push Rodney's chair over to the small park across the street. It looked like it should be somewhat quieter than the pandemonium that surrounded the explosion area.

"That's fine. When he wants to return to the manor house let me know and I'll have a bobby drive him. I'll be around to talk with him again as soon as we get this sorted out." He looked over the scene, which stretched in all directions.

I looked at the mangle that used to be Rodney's huge Suburban. It had taken well-placed and heavy explosives to blow it up. The air still smelled of burning metal and rubber. Bloody pieces of body were splattered throughout the area. It was going to take several hours for the forensics team to do their jobs. The press had arrived in force and I noticed one especially attractive blonde trying her best to engage DC Johnston in conversation. He wasn't cooperating. It looked as if the English press was as aggressive as what I'd seen in Las Vegas.

"I'm going to push you across the street, Rodney, then I'd like to hear what happened. Are you up to it?" I asked, looking to see if he was going into shock. "Have you been checked out by the medics?"

"Yes, and I'm doing as well as can be expected. They wanted to haul me away to hospital but I refused. That's when I asked for you to come down here. DC Johnston has been grand, considering the situation."

"Then I'm going to move you away from this and we can talk." I went behind the chair and easily pushed him the short distance. I turned the chair so he faced the park. We could hear the grisly business that was going on but at least didn't have to look at what was left of his car.

I sat down on a park bench and faced Rodney. The investigation was well under way. I watched as a white van with Coroner written on the side made its way slowly through the throng of people. The perimeter had been roped off by blue and white police tape and the officers were pushing back the pack of wolves that called themselves "the press." It pleased me that no one had noticed our departure from the area. However, I knew that would end once the press put the story together.

"Can you tell me what happened, Rodney?"

"Yes, I can tell you exactly what occurred. It should have been me who was blown to bits, not Michael." He covered his eyes and bent forward. "I asked him if he'd bring the van around to the front. I always park in the back. He's driven my Suburban many times and knew how to operate all the gadgets." He pulled his hands away from his eyes and sat up straight in the wheel chair. Tears ran down his thin cheeks and he wiped them away before he continued. "The bomb was set to go off after the van had been driven a ways. It's what we British troops went through in Northern Ireland – the same sort of scenario. I don't understand, May, why do these people want me dead?" His eyes looked tortured and I realized he must have been re-living the horror he went through when he lost his legs long ago in Northern Ireland.

"It has to do with your inheritance, just as DC Johnston said in our meeting, but why this method was chosen, I don't know. Will you be all right while I go across the street for a moment?"

Rodney barely nodded his head. His forehead was covered in sweat and he was shivering. I took my jacket off and wrapped it around his thin shoulders.

I walked quickly across the street and interrupted a conversation DC Johnston was having with a uniformed officer.

"We need to get Rodney out of here and into the nearest hospital. He's going into shock, I believe."

"Yes, alright. I tried to get him to leave before but he refused. I'll get the medical techs to take him in their vehicle."

I went back to be with Rodney and, within five minutes, he was bundled up and gently placed into the van. The action alerted the press to another source of information. They swarmed me as the medical vehicle drove slowly through the street, lights flashing and siren on.

Chapter Fourteen

"Leave her alone. She has nothing to do with this case," DC Johnston said in an authoritarian voice. The press had descended on me like ducks on a June bug and I was glad he was doing his best to ferret me away from their abuse. "Come stand with me, May, behind the tape. They won't be able to get at you there."

"Thanks, I'll accept your offer. They're worse than anything I've seen in Las Vegas."

Before he could comment, the blonde woman I'd noticed earlier screamed, "Is she your new girlfriend, Johnston?" Everybody in the press corps laughed so it must have been funny but DC Johnston looked like he could kill the lot of them.

"Please excuse the rude behavior of my countrymen – and women. I wish I could tell you it will get better, but it will truly get much worse. They're like a pack of black-back jackals, as you might have noticed." He pulled me toward the tape and lifted it so I could get under.

"Did Lord Willsdon tell you anything I need to know before he left for hospital?" DC Johnston asked, as he continued to survey the scene.

"I guess you already knew he'd asked Michael to drive his van around from the back of the law office to the street. Do you have any idea why? Before I could question him further, he began to show signs of shock."

"Actually, yes. The receptionist said Lord Willsdon was talking with another of the solicitors in the firm and asked Mr. Reed to bring it around. They had decided to go to the pub for a quick bite after the meeting ended. Let's go to my car so we can have privacy and continue our talk."

The detective led me to a large, black SUV that he'd parked away from the crime scene. Unless he'd told me, I'd never have guessed it was a police vehicle. There were no markings on the outside and when I opened the heavy door and sat down, the smell of expensive leather overwhelmed me.

He had stopped to talk with a young motorcycle officer so I had a few moments to be nosy. The inside of the car was spotless. I lifted my feet off the mat to make sure I hadn't brought any dirt or grass in with me. There wasn't a police radio or computer in sight. I knew that Las Vegas police cars used the computer as a "second officer." I didn't like it and it certainly wasn't how I had been trained when I entered "the thin blue line" as a young patrol officer in Tacoma, Washington. As a rookie, I had been assigned to work with a seasoned officer who showed me the ropes and introduced me around the unit and other sectors. I learned more from him than I ever did in any training class.

The driver door on the right opened and DC Johnston got in, slamming it harder than necessary. "I envy you, May," he said as he looked at me. "I get so tired of this nonsense. I've just been called on the carpet because of my 'tone' with that telly news reporter. Just give me a moment to send an email to 'explain' my actions."

He reached under the console and pulled out a sleek computer that was attached to a swivel base and placed it on an armrest that he pulled down from the center section of the bench seat. He opened the laptop and started typing.

I watched him and chuckled.

"Can you share the joke?" he asked, pausing in mid-keystroke.

"Finish your email and I'll explain."

He spent a few minutes composing the 'mea culpa' message and hit send with a sigh. "I'm not sure I believe all this media openness and free speech is a good idea," he said as he closed up the laptop and stowed it underneath the console.

"They have their place. I just wish it was somewhere far away from law enforcement," I commented with a grin.

"Amen to that. Now, what was so funny?"

"I was pleased that you didn't have a computer in the car when I got in and had a look around. Then you pull out this space-age laptop. I miss the days when there were two officers in the car; don't you?"

"Yes and no. I find I can get more done when I don't have some sniveling youngster to train."

"Well, having been one of those 'snivelers,' I think it's the best way to get a young officer off to a good start."

"The next time I'm saddled with one, I'll call you up to take over for me," DC Johnston said.

I nodded in agreement. He smiled as he'd said it but I knew he really didn't like being tied down. "Would you rather talk with me some other time? I know you have much to do and a minimum time to do it."

"No, I need to go back over what you've told me. And I thought we'd drive to hospital to see how Lord Willsdon is doing," he replied.

"Good, I'd like to do that. Where do you want me to start?" I asked, as he started the car.

"Start with your morning at the cottage, before you came into the village for the meeting."

He backed out of the tight quarters and got the car turned around and we headed for the nearest hospital, which was located in Swindon. I'd noticed it when Rodney had taken me to the university that he worked for on a part-time basis.

The day had turned out to be beautiful and I retold the events of the morning as we sped along the narrow road that would take us past Stonehenge on the way to Rodney.

"I notice you're not taking the freeway. This is the same way I came with Rodney when he brought me over to see where he worked. It's the 'tourist road,' according to what he told me. Is this the fastest way to get to Swindon from the village?" I wanted to get there as quickly as possible. Even though the road took us past Stonehenge and it was an awe-inspiring sight, I knew that Rodney needed someone to be with him.

"I had a report that there was a lorry overturned on the motorway so thought this would be the better route. It's usually the tourist buses that make it a slow-go through here but so far, so good," he commented as we followed the road around the curves of Salisbury Plain.

This was the third time I'd seen Stonehenge since coming to England. It sent chills up my spine to realize the history and legends of the place that looked, in person, even eerier than any photos I'd seen of it. It looked smaller than I'd pictured, and more ancient. As I thought this, Sarah's image popped into my head and I could have sworn I heard her say, "Help me."

I looked at DC Johnston and asked if he'd said something to me.

"No, you seemed to be in your own reverie and I didn't want to disturb you. Anyway, you've had quite a shock yourself today. Let's don't forget that you might have been in that car instead of Mr. Reed."

Now that he'd brought it up, I realized that could be true. "But there's no reason to harm me. I'm just a tourist here for a summer holiday."

"You told me yourself that you don't trust most of Lord Willsdon's friends. There had to be something about them that made you wary. Also, and this is just a quirk, but something I've noticed. Usually, the English don't readily accept foreigners, even Americans; we tend to be a 'stand-offish' breed. Yet here you are, in the midst of this small village, mucking about and picking up clues left and right. And you're making noises about a cold case from forty-plus years ago. I'm an English lad and I've certainly not been allowed access into village life as you have done." Detective Johnston drove expertly along the road as he delivered this personality analysis I didn't like.

I looked at him and I'm sure the aggravation showed on my face. "Don't you think it has something to do with the fact that I'm renting a cottage from the local pooh-bah, Lord-High-Everything-Else, toff, boss, whatever Rodney is considered to be in these parts? He's the reason I'm accepted. And another thing – something you should know full well as a seasoned police officer. It's not uncommon for the police to be outsiders. Good grief, you should have picked that up as soon as you put on the uniform."

"You're sputtering like a wet hen," he laughed.

Chapter Fifteen

By the time we'd arrived at the hospital in Swindon, I'd gotten beyond my irritation at Detective Johnston. He was, after all, doing his job and I knew how difficult that could be. One thing he didn't need was another irritant. The important thing was to find – and quickly – who was responsible for the death of Solicitor Michael Reed. I also was worried about Rodney and how this might affect his long-term physical and mental well-being.

The two-story hospital appeared old, built of the yellowish-stone I associated with the Cotswold's. Of course, the famous villages of the Cotswold limestone hills were just a little north of where I stood. I made a promise to visit several of them before I left England.

Once inside, the Matron led us to Rodney's room, which was located on the first floor. She tapped on the door and swung it open. "How's Lord Willsdon doing now?" she boomed out in a too-loud voice. It made me wonder if she might be hard of hearing.

Rodney looked small and frail in the stark white-covered bed. There weren't any windows in the room and it reminded me of a monk's cell I'd seen once on a trip to Italy.

"Oh, my," he said, "the cavalry has come to rescue me."

"I like that answer. And how are you doing? Are you ready to get out of here?"

"Yes, May, let's go now," he said as he pushed himself into a sitting position. "I can leave, can't I, Matron?"

She shook her head in a negative fashion. "No, Lord Willsdon. Maybe tomorrow. The Doctor has ordered tests and we need results before we can release you."

"They think I suffered a wee heart attack. Can you believe that?" Rodney asked, his eyes wide with disbelief.

The detective hadn't said anything since we'd entered the room. He stood near the door, observing Rodney. "Do you know why anyone would want to blow up your car, Lord Willsdon?" he asked.

"No, and I'm not sure it was blown up. Maybe there was something wrong with the petrol and it was an accident. Maybe someone threw a lighted fag on the street and the car caught fire. It doesn't have to mean that someone tried to kill me."

"I didn't say someone did. I asked who would want to blow up your car," the detective responded. "Do you think someone wants to kill you?"

Rodney seemed to shrink back into the pillow. "No, I don't believe that for a minute."

By the way he had answered, I knew Rodney thought that was exactly what had happened. "Could it be related to those letters you've received?" I asked. "It was pretty clear they want you to give up your title and estate, 'for the good of the village,' if I recall the wording correctly."

The Matron stepped in and stopped our questioning, which I agreed with. Rodney had been through enough for one day. I should have known better, but I got caught up in acting like an inquisitor, not the friend he needed me to be. "I'll bring Jazz to the cottage and he can stay with me until you get home tomorrow," I said, trying to make amends.

"Thank you, May. I would appreciate that. Please take him for a walk, if you have the time."

"I'll make time for Jazz," I said as I squeezed Rodney's hand, which was cold to the touch.

"We'll return tomorrow, Lord Willsdon. Matron, a moment, please?"

When we got into the hall, Detective Johnston asked about the prognosis. "Do you think he'll be ready for more questioning tomorrow? Was it a serious heart attack or a warning?"

I thought that was an interesting question. Weren't all heart attacks serious? The Matron answered, "As I said, tests are to be completed later today and we should have results tomorrow. I'll give you my number and you can ring me midday."

She led us toward the main door, stopping by the large central counter to pick up two cards – one for each of us. "I'll expect your call, Detective," she said as she ushered us out the door.

"What was that business about a 'warning' heart attack?" I asked, as we made our way to the police car.

"It might turn out to be the onset of angina, which is something I know all about. I've been under care for that for several years now," he said as he opened the door for me.

"Oh," I replied. When he got settled in I asked, "So have you had a 'warning'?"

"Yes. Now, let's get off that subject. Are you hungry?"

"Always," I replied honestly.

"How about the Prince and Pauper for a pub meal? "

"I think I smell more investigating coming our way."

"Yes, well, I'm taking it seriously that you are suspicious of the owner's motives toward Lord Willsdon. I believe she's the buxom blonde named Leslie Waters Sumac, daughter of the late Mrs. Angelina Waters, renowned as the village witch."

"And Steven Roberts is still in love with Mrs. Waters," I said.

"Do tell," DC Johnston replied.

So I told him about my strange encounter with Steven in the cemetery.

The road back to the village was busy with late afternoon tourists on the way to see Stonehenge. By the time we'd crawled past the line of busses and cars waiting to get into the parking area, I was ready to eat anything that came my way.

Thankfully, the parking sites were all but empty at the Prince and Pauper. I was glad to get out of the car and stretch. It had taken twice as long to return to the village because of the slow traffic.

Inside, it didn't take Leslie but a few moments to discover who had come to sample her wares, so to speak.

"Well, look who's here," she said gaily, blonde curls tumbling down. The tops of her round breasts protruded from a shocking pink peasant top. A gold-colored cinched belt circled her small waistline and a billowy black skirt reached almost to the floor. Gold spike heels completed the outfit. She reminded me of some of the ''ladies of the evening'' we used to arrest on the streets near the Strip in Las Vegas.

After we were seated, items selected off the short menu, and with a cup of real coffee in front of me, I asked Detective Johnston for his thoughts about Leslie.

"She reminds me of some of the tarts we regularly rounded up in the west end of London," he said and then took a long drink of pale ale. "I'm off duty, by the way," he explained.

"Has she ever been arrested for anything?"

"No, not a thing. In fact, none of Lord Willsdon's friends have a criminal record. All clean as a whistle."

I sipped my coffee and looked around at the beautifully decorated pub, which was spotless. "It's almost as though she's playing a part, isn't it?" I asked.

"I don't know. But you have a feeling about it so I'll trust that."

"Wow, I never heard any of my partners anywhere say that before. They all thought I was nuts when I got one of my 'flashes.'"

"My mother is 'that way' so I respect it." He pulled his cell phone from his jacket pocket, looked at the identifying name, and excused himself. "I'll be back momentarily," he explained.

While he answered the call, Leslie came over with a basket filled with fresh bread and butter to munch on. She pulled out a chair and sat down while I buttered a warm roll. "What's this I hear about our Rodney? Is it true his car was blown up? I saw it on the telly but I couldn't get the sound turned up fast enough to hear what was said."

I was on my second roll by the time she had asked her question. "Yes, it's true. Detective Johnston and I just came back from seeing him at the hospital. He's okay but will stay overnight for more tests." I purposely left out the part about the suspected heart attack. My hand reached into the basket for another roll when the detective came back.

"Oh, hello again, Mrs. Sumac," he said as he sat down. "I see May has eaten most of the rolls already."

"I rarely see a woman eat like that. It's refreshing," she commented. "And please, call me Leslie. Makes me feel old to hear the 'Mrs.' part. Anyway, he's long gone."

"Divorce?" I asked nosily, as I buttered the last roll in the basket.

"No, he died. Let me go get more rolls, since May has consumed them all." She took the basket and headed toward the kitchen.

"Sorry about that, but I was starved."

"Don't worry about it. Here comes another basketful."

Leslie set them down on the table next to the detective. "I thought he should at least have one roll before you take over, May. I have to go visit my regulars; if you need anything else, let me know. Your meals will be up in a few minutes." She walked over to another table where a group of men awaited her arrival.

"Did you know her husband was dead?" I sipped my coffee to try to get my mind off the soft, warm yeast rolls.

"These really are good. I should come in here more often," he commented. "Yes, I knew about the late Mr. Sumac. He was an old man when she married him. And guess what? She inherited all of his money, land, and this business. She's probably the wealthiest woman in the village."

"Was an inquest held?"

"It was ruled 'natural causes' as he died at home, had previous health problems, and was in his eighties." He took a sip of the ale and watched Leslie as she charmed the men.

"So she was, what, in her twenties when she married him?"

"Actually, she was a teenager."

"My, my, little Leslie Waters Sumac set herself up for life, didn't she?"

"If you take the cynical view, yes. She married him a few days after her mother passed. And of course, she'd left Leslie all of her worldly goods, too, which were considerable." He munched on a second roll then slid the basket toward me. "Go ahead, finish them off. I'm tired of you watching every bite that goes in my mouth."

"No, I'm going to be good...okay, just one more, then I'm through."

"It's said the way to a man's heart is through his stomach so maybe that's what the old boy saw in our Leslie," Detective Johnston said.

We both watched Leslie as she leaned over so the men could get a good look at her assets. "You think?" I asked, as I buttered the last roll.

Chapter Sixteen

DC Johnston dropped me off in front of the cottage. "I'll call you tomorrow, as soon as I've spoken with Matron about Lord Willsdon's condition." He waved good-bye and drove off.

I dug around in my purse for the key, and then unlocked the front door of the cottage. I went into the bedroom and changed from a skirt to my jeans. It hadn't taken long to realize that slacks weren't worn in England as casually as in the States. I copied their fashion and only wore jeans around the cottage and when I took Jazz for walks, which I was about to do. I left by way of the back door, locking it securely. The key was tucked into my jeans pocket, which I noticed felt tighter than usual. "Too many rolls," I muttered to myself.

The walk to Rodney's estate took less than five minutes. I went around back and knocked on the door that led into the kitchen. No one answered so I slowly opened it and called a hello. It seemed unnaturally quiet as I took a step inside. About that time Jazz came bounding up to me. "Were you asleep in your little doggie room?" I asked as I ruffled his silky ears. Rodney had shown me where Jazz slept the first time I'd come to the house for tea and volunteered to take the Border collie for "walkies," as he'd termed it.

"Come on, Jazz, let's go walk off some of that big lunch I just finished."

He wagged his entire body, and his plumy tail did a definite joyous dance. He pranced around and bounded outside as soon as I opened the door for him. He had a "doggie door" but he was such a social animal that he much preferred to have companionship when he went outside.

"You need sheep to herd, Jazz. Let's go find some for you to stare at."

He knew exactly what I meant because he ran off in the direction of the farmer and sheep we had seen on our first walk together. I followed along, going faster than I would have liked, but enjoying it just the same. He was in front, leading the way to the open field where the herd spent the day munching the green grass. Huge trees sheltered me from the sun, which was beginning to set. A soft breeze blew and I smelled the loamy earth as we traveled through the forest. The square church tower was in the distance so I knew we were approaching the field. The church stone looked like the same type used to build the Swindon hospital. This was a lovely approach to the village. It looked like the photos I'd seen in travel brochures and on-line which had made me select this part of England in which to spend my holiday.

Jazz ran back and jumped around in excited circles. "You want me to hurry up, don't you, boy?" I said to him. Getting down one knee, I wrapped my arms around his neck and put my face in his black and white fur. "I have to tell you something, Jazz. Rodney is sick and won't be home for awhile. I'll take care of you while he's gone, though. I promised him I'd walk you every day and you can stay with me in the little cottage. Is that okay with you, boy?" He licked my face then lifted his left paw and waved it at me. "I guess that means it's okay. Now, let's go find those sheep."

We traveled a little farther and there they were, like a charming, pastoral picture painted on canvas. This was the reason I had come to England.

We watched the farmer and his dog herd the reluctant sheep back through the gate so they could go home for the night. The dog ran and corralled them into a rag-tag line, finally getting the stragglers through the wooden gate. The farmer waved his staff to us as he left, and I waved back at him. I'd have to ask Rodney who he was. His hair was white and he was dressed in overalls that reminded me a little of my grandfather. He'd raised me after my parents had been killed long ago on a rain-slick Montana highway. The man who had run them off the road had been drunk. The first time I'd ever ridden in a police vehicle was the night I was picked up at the football game, where I was one of the cheerleaders for our high school team. The officers were kind as they drove my grandfather and me to the morgue to identify my parents, who had been on their way to the game. After that my life had changed. I lived with my grandfather on his Montana ranch and as soon as I graduated from school, I applied for and was accepted into the Tacoma Police Department as a rookie cop. My grandfather had cried when I left him, but he understood I had to have my own life, and I knew it wasn't going to be in Montana. It had always been too cold for me there.

Jazz's whining brought me out of my reverie. I shook my head to bring the present back where it belonged. I wiped the tears from my face and said, "Come on, Jazz, let's go pack your doggie bag so you can stay with me."

He stayed close by my side, not running off and leaving me behind. With his canine insight, he knew that I needed a loving companion at that moment.

We took our time getting back, circling through a part of the forest I hadn't explored yet. I saw lights on at the estate so knew someone must have come back. It seemed unusual that such a big estate wouldn't have someone around all the time. I knew Mrs. Long didn't stay over, but I thought Rodney had told me someone from his staff lived on the estate with him. I'd clarify that with him tomorrow when we saw him at the hospital.

As we approached the back of the estate, I paused for a moment and looked over the grounds and the glistening lake. Ducks and swans floated lazily on the water. Rhododendrons and azalea, in full bloom, grew alongside the water. A chestnut tree had purple wisteria growing up its trunk. The clusters of blossoms hanging down in rope-like fashion from the limbs made it look like an enormous grape vine.

Reluctantly, I turned back to the house. The weather was too beautiful to go inside, I thought.

"Come on, Jazz, the party's over. Let's go get your goodies. Then you can sit with me while I take a long, soaking bath. We won't think about the fact that a young girl died in there and shows up sometimes, even though she's been dead for about forty years or so." He sat patiently and listened to me talk.

I knocked on the door again and no one answered. We went inside and I rummaged around for a piece of paper and a pen so I could write a note to the staff, to let them know I had Jazz at the cottage. Then I found a paper sack for the dog food. "This will be for your breakfast. Do you want some food and water now, boy?" I asked as he looked at me with those melting-chocolate-brown eyes. I filled his water bowl and put a little food in his dish. He gobbled it up, so I added more. He took a few slurps of water then ate the rest. "My, you're hungry. I wonder when you were fed last?"

Jazz stopped eating, his ears perked up and he started barking and making noises in the back of his throat that reminded me of wolf sounds like I'd heard on National Geographic. "Wow, has your personality changed," I said.

He lunged into the dark hallway and I followed. "Jazz, what are you doing, boy?" I asked, not wanting to know the answer. I heard his paws as they skidded on the slick marble. He was barking furiously and I was feeling along the walls trying to find a light switch. Someone had turned on the lights in the back, but the front of the huge house was dark. The sun hadn't set but it was twilight and with the heavy curtains on the leaded windows, it seemed dark anyway. Sunlight never really penetrated the gloom of this place, I thought, as I frantically sought light. I found a large lamp and turned it on. I was delighted that it actually worked. Jazz was scrabbling with his front paws under the double doors of the room I had been in a few days before. I went over and opened them and he immediately raced into the large room. I found the round push-in light switch, and light flooded the entire area. I looked where Jazz stood, barking non-stop. There was a body lying on the floor behind the sofa. I knew that because I saw a hand, palm up, in plain sight. I took a step and then heard someone walking behind me. Before I could turn and see who was there, Jazz raced forward and in a leap knocked the person down who was directly behind me. I couldn't believe that sweet-natured Jazz could make such horrifying noises. I reached to pull him off before he ripped the person apart.

My ex-husband, Dan, lay on the floor, covered by the dog. When I saw who it was, it ran through my mind that I should let Jazz finish him off.

"Get Cujo off me!" Dan yelled, as I pulled Jazz back.

"That's okay, boy, he's sort of a good guy. You can stop growling now." I calmed Jazz down and petted him.

"If you'd treated me that good I never would have run off with that dim-bat secretary of mine," Dan commented, as he stood up.

"You were never as nice to me as Jazz is," I countered. "Anyway, before you explain to me what you're doing here, we have a slight problem."

"What's that?" he asked as he glanced around the room. "Don't tell me there's another pooch in this mausoleum that's going to attack me."

"There's a body behind the couch and I think it's a dead body."

Dan, ever the coward, jumped back and headed out the door and Jazz immediately stood up and started growling. "Whoa, boys, both of you calm down. Let's have a look"

I got up and walked around the couch, there to find the very dead body of the late Mrs. Long, Rodney's housekeeper. From the looks of it she had been shot. Her eyes were open and there was a look of disbelief on her face, as if she couldn't believe who was doing this terrible thing.

Jazz came over and stood by me. "Is there really a dead person in there?" Dan asked from the hall, where he'd retreated.

"Yes, now call the police. I don't want to touch anything in here more than we already have," I said and went out to join him. "And then I want a full explanation of why you're following me around like a stalker."

Dan called the number I gave him and told the police about the murder.

"I've been here a week and so far I've seen two murders, one of which involved a car bomb. And I live with a ghost," I said as we waited in the kitchen for the Scene of Crime Officers to arrive.

"Yes, well, there's lots of crime in America, too, don't forget," Dan said. "I've just read some stats that said Las Vegas has more crime than anywhere else in the States, which is another reason I don't understand why you live there."

"Touché," I commented, and waited for DC Johnston.

Chapter Seventeen

When I heard the police cars turn onto the estate road, I took Jazz and we walked around to the front of the manor to wait for them. I left Dan shivering in the kitchen.

The crime scene personnel tumbled out of their van like white-suited space aliens and headed for the massive front doors. I was about to tell them it was locked but they opened it with no problem. They were followed by the coroner, who rumbled up in an old but gorgeous British racing green MGB, top down, his blond hair blowing in the wind. Behind him the coroner's white van, driven by his female assistant, screeched to a halt beside the sports car. I remembered him and his MGB from the car bomb crime scene. He and his staff had a busy week, I thought.

When the ambulance drove up and the two men climbed out of their vehicle, I asked if they'd take a look at Dan, too. "I think he may need something to calm him down," I said. They followed the other officers who were starting to make the place look like the set of crime dramas I've seen on the BBC. I looked around to see if Inspector Lynley and Sergeant Havers were lurking somewhere on the premises.

"Are you looking for me?" DC Johnston said as he walked up.

"Sort of," I replied. "Sorry about this, Detective. You don't get much time off, do you?"

"And this is your holiday, let's not forget that. How is it you can get involved in so many murders in such a short time?" he asked as he took his phone out of his jacket pocket.

"I don't know. Luck of the Irish?" I replied.

"Excuse me while I take this," he commented and moved away from me.

Jazz and I watched the drama unfold for a few more minutes then walked back to the kitchen. I found Dan surrounded by the medical technicians. He kept trying to swat their hands away. "I'm alright, leave me alone."

"Dan, let them help you." I said, "You know you don't handle these things well. I don't want you passing out." I went over and tried to talk sense into him, which I knew was a waste of my time.

I walked over to the enormous kitchen cabinets, opened a few of them until I found what I was looking for, then got a bottle of stout from the shelf and took it over to Dan. "I'll find an opener for you," I said then turned toward the kitchen.

"Don't bother, I'll just twist it off. Isn't there a cold one somewhere? I don't like this room temperature crap," Dan complained.

"They think icy cold drinks are bad for your digestion. Get over it. Now, let's talk about why you're in England, breaking and entering into a manor house and stalking me. Any comments, Dan?" I asked as he swilled down the beer.

"I'm not stalking you. I came to tell you I met that blonde woman at the pub. Yeah, she might have been my type a few hundred years ago, but not now. You are," he said and wiggled his eyebrows at me.

When I didn't comment, he continued. "I stopped by your place and when you didn't answer and your Land Rover was parked outside, I thought you were close by. I saw lights from a car coming out of the woods, so after it had turned onto the highway, I took the road it was on and wound up here."

"So you came down the road that's beside the cottage?" I asked, confused by his description.

"No, I told you. I came down the road that goes through the woods. Didn't you know about it?"

"Obviously not, Dan. I have no idea what road you're talking about." How had I missed it, I wondered. Jazz and I had been in the woods that very afternoon and hadn't seen another road.

"Can you show me?" I asked him.

"Sure, let's go." He got up and headed for the back door.

"Wait for Jazz and me. I have to let the detective know what we're doing."

"Don't tell me you have to kowtow to these cops. You're not even part of the force. Why should they care if you go for a walk in the woods with your husband? And let's leave Cujo behind, too. That dog is nasty," Dan said.

"One more word about Jazz and I'll never speak to you again," I threatened. "And it's protocol with the detective. Now sit back down and wait for me," I ordered.

"Yes, ma'am, Ms. Police Officer," he jeered, and then sat down.

I walked into the hallway, now ablaze with light, and found DC Johnston with the coroner. "Detective, I wanted to let you know I'll be outside. My ex told me he saw a car coming from the manor house and then he came up that road to find me. The thing is, I didn't know the road existed, so I'm going to look for it. We'll be careful and won't trample tire marks."

"No, don't do that," he said. "Let me assemble a forensics team to get out there. He can show all of us what he saw. Give me five minutes, please."

I nodded agreement and went back to the kitchen to wait.

True to his word, the detective and a couple of team members joined us in a few minutes. We walked outside, Jazz close to me, and followed Dan as he led us to the side road. "Here it is," he gestured. "I saw the car lights from the cottage and followed the road back here."

"Okay, let's get some lights and check it out," Detective Johnston said. The team members walked toward the front of the manor to gather their equipment.

"Tell me, Mr. - I'm afraid I don't recall your name, sir," the detective said to Dan.

"I'm Eva May's husband," he replied.

"Ex-husband," I corrected.

Detective Johnston looked at us. "Yes, I'm aware of that. And your name, sir?"

"Dan Peterman."

"Well, Mr. Peterman, are you a Las Vegas police officer as is Ms. Scott?"

"No, that's never been my gig," Dan replied.

"What is your 'gig,' sir?" He asked pointedly. "Why are you in England, and more precisely, how did you get into Lord Willsdon's home?"

Before Dan could answer, the forensics team came back with their equipment and lit up the road as if it was daylight.

"Yes, well, we can follow that line of questioning in a few moments. Please, Mr. Peterman, explain where you were and what exactly did you see?" The detective asked as he kneeled down and looked for tire marks.

"I told you already. How many times do I have to say the same thing?" Dan whined.

"Just answer the questions," I said, getting more aggravated by the minute. "You're bad for my blood pressure."

Dan sighed. "I never should have come over here. I didn't think you'd be so mean about it, though, May."

To get away from him, I walked over to one of the white-suited team members and looked around the narrow road. "I can't believe I've walked past this road several times and never saw it."

"Don't feel bad, Miss, I've lived here my whole life and never knew it was here," the young man replied. "Please put these on," he asked and handed me a pair white shoe covers.

"It will be like looking for that haystack with the needle in it, won't it?" I asked him, as I put them over my tennis shoes.

"Yes, Miss. This will be a rare hard find. Leaves from the oak trees are everywhere. You'd have to know about this road to be able to follow the track"

"Thanks for letting me tag along," I said to him.

"DC Johnston said you were one of us, only from across the pond," he replied with a big smile.

The team moved methodically down the constricted road. I followed along, waiting for Detective Johnston to call me back. When I looked, he and Dan were deep in discussion. I couldn't imagine that Dan had anything so interesting to say. I had been surprised by his comments about Leslie Sumac, however. I would have bet that she would have been his dream girl.

The road took a turn and we lost sight of the manor house. The dense forest shrouded Dan and the detective. It felt eerie even though police personnel surrounded me and the way was brightly lit.

We continued slowly to make our way to the main road, looking for evidence. When I saw where the hidden track came out, I was surprised.

My cottage was to the right and the small garden shed that was in such disrepair was located next to the hidden road.

The night was quiet and all of us stood there looking at where we had come out of the woods. Even though I now knew where the road started, it wouldn't have been at all evident. If Dan hadn't seen the car lights, he would have followed the main road to the manor house, which was on the other side of the cottage.

"Are you sure," I asked the young officer, "that you didn't know about this road? I would think you would have been all over these woods when you were younger."

He looked around, and then stood with hands on his hips. "No, ma'am, I never did. Part of it is that we were sternly warned away by the toffs who live in the manor house. They made it plain we weren't wanted on the estate."

My puzzlement showed on my face as he continued with his comments. "I recall one Hallows Eve when a group of lads from the village sneaked onto the grounds. We didn't get too far when the dogs were let loose on us."

"Dogs?" I asked. "The only one I've seen is the Border collie and no one would be afraid of him. Except my crazy ex-husband, that is," I added.

"No, they were big dogs. I don't know if they're still here or not. Maybe when the current Lord Willsdon took over he got rid of them. It kept us away, though. I thought they'd tear us apart. But it worked – we never came back. In fact, this is the first time since then I've set foot on this place." He looked around then added, "I'll join my mates, now, miss. Thanks for your help." He walked back toward the gaggle of officers who continued to sift through the leaves, trying to find some clue as to the make of car, tire thread or any evidence that would send them in a logical direction to solve the murder of Mrs. Long.

The night air was still and the stars twinkled in the clear sky. Because there were no streetlights, the stars seemed to shine brighter. No cars traveled the road and it was quiet enough for me to hear cricket noises and frogs. It sounded like any wooded area at night and it seemed peaceful to me.

I continued to look around the edge of the roadway then turned back toward the manor house. A series of flashes caught my attention and I walked around the slightly curved road toward them. As I went deeper into the woods, and off the road, I saw the bright work lights of the scene of crime team through the thick grove of trees. They were congregated in a circle around a small area that had bushes around it.

I walked over to join them. Two of the team members kneeled beside an area and gingerly removed the top layer of dirt away. As they worked, it became clear what they had found. A bone emerged from their careful digging and it was placed next to other bone fragments on a piece of white plastic that lay next to them. Another officer clicked away with the camera, which had created the flashes that led me to them. As I moved closer I was surprised to see that the bushes were actually roses, with their buds just unfurling. They looked as though they had been tended, and recently. I looked at the stem edges and they were cleanly pruned.

DC Johnston walked up. "What have you found?" he asked to no one in particular.

One of the officers who had been digging looked around and said, "It's human remains, sir. And they've been here for awhile."

Chapter Eighteen

Detective Constable Johnston sent me back to the manor house to tell Dan we were free to go. As I approached the house I saw him leaning against one of the concrete lions that guarded the enormous wooden front doors. I could understand how so many of the English estate owners had either sold and got out or opened their palatial homes to the public. Upkeep must be a financial nightmare. It made me wonder how Rodney's family had managed to keep it a private estate. I would have to ask him that when I saw him later in the day, for I realized it was now well past midnight.

"Eva May, I'm going back to the States. And if you'll listen to me, you'll join me. This place gives me the creeps," Dan said, as he puffed away on one of his cigarettes.

I walked closer to him then started waving my arms to move the smoke away from my face. "I thought you'd given up those things." I asked. "Stop smoking now or I'll just turn around and leave."

He took the cigarette out of his mouth, used his fingers to put out the lighted end, and then stuck it in his pocket. "Satisfied? And I did stop until I got here. Leave with me, May. This place isn't safe. How do you keep landing in situations where people get killed? Do you draw it to you or something?"

I looked around at the buzz of activity. A TV news van was coming toward us and as I looked closer I saw that the same female reporter who had complained about DC Johnston was in the passenger seat.

"Let's get out of here, Dan. Follow me," I urged. "Where is Jazz?"

"You think I keep up with that killer-dog? I hope I never see him again. Why are you so nervous all of a sudden? You can see a dead body

111

and not bat an eye but a news van drives up and you start hyperventilating," he said, grinning.

"I'll explain later. Let's go around the side of the house." I walked as fast as I could without running and Dan followed, mercifully with his mouth shut.

We went around to the side, halfway to the back of the huge old house, and found a steep stairway. At the top of the steps there was a door that I was sure would be locked. When I tried the curved handle, I was surprised that it opened easily and we followed the wide passageway toward the sound of voices. Thick rugs covered the stone floor and lighted wall sconces highlighted paintings that, as I glanced at them as we rushed past, looked like family portraits from long ago. A pocket door took the two of us to figure out but we eventually found the hidden latch.

"You forgot to tell me, why are we running?" Dan asked as we stepped into the huge foyer.

"Later," I said, as I slid the door closed behind us. As I did so, the passageway effectively disappeared.

"Look, Dan, it's invisible." I stood and stared at the wooden panel that blended in with the rest of the wall. "How would we get it open again?" I asked, searching again for the hidden latch that wasn't in the same place as on the other side of the panel.

"Yeah, groovy. Now, let's pack up and get out of here," he said as he started walking toward the back of the house.

"If they want it to be a secret passageway, why are there steps outside the house?" I asked to Dan's retreating back.

He turned around and said, "Geez, May, leave it alone. I'm telling you, you draw this stuff to you. Give it up and let's get out of this mausoleum."

"Let's find the latch. It's not where it should be."

Grumbling, he came over and helped. We searched around before we discovered that it was at the bottom of the panel and was almost impossible to make out. As we worked on it, I realized it looked exactly like the bottom of the airline cart I'd tried to figure out a few days earlier. "Thanks, Dan, I couldn't have solved this mystery without you."

"See? I can be of some use. You need to start appreciating my good side, Eva May."

"Don't get your knickers in a twist, I appreciate your good side. It's just that you so rarely show it," I responded.

We walked back to the kitchen, which had turned into the headquarters for the investigation. Jazz was curled up under the big, wooden table, but crawled out from underneath it and came over to me as soon as we came in the door. The rest of the busy team members ignored us as they rushed on with their work.

"DC Johnston said we could leave, by the way," I told Dan.

"Ah, finally, a voice of reason. Let's go," he said, heading for the back door.

"Okay, but first I need to gather some things for Jazz. Can you help me carry his dog food and dish? Oh, and we should get his bed, too. It's in the side room, over there," I pointed.

"If this will get you out of here, I'll carry that mutt myself," Dan said.

"Wait here while I go speak with the police officer," I told him.

The officer was young and was busy searching through an old oak desk. "Can I help you, Miss?" he asked when I walked up to him.

"Is it okay for me to take the dog and some of his things to the cottage, since this is still a crime scene?" I asked.

"I'm afraid not, Miss, for the reasons you just gave," he answered, as he continued to search through the large desk that sat in a hall way just off the kitchen area.

"I promised Lord Willsdon I'd look after his dog since he's in the hospital. Would you check to see if I could just take him? I could get food and such at the market tomorrow." By this time, Dan had wandered over and eavesdropped on the conversation.

I had baffled the officer with that question, as he replied, "Let me ask about that, Miss. Stay right here for a moment, please." He disappeared into the front of the house, I presumed to ask someone of higher rank what to do with the bothersome American tourist who kept asking questions as he'd tried to work.

Dan gazed down at his feet and shuffled them.

"Okay, what's going on, Dan?" I asked knowing he wanted to say something that I wasn't going to like.

Dan looked at me and said, "I can't figure out why this guy, Lord Willsdon, doesn't have friends who are taking care of his pooch. Why are you doing that anyway? He's got servants, lived here all his life and you're the one who's taking care of things. It doesn't make any sense to me, May, that's all."

I hadn't really thought about it that way, but now that Dan had brought it up, he had a point. "I don't know. Maybe I should find out," I replied.

The officer came back and said it was okay to take Jazz with me. Dan and I walked down the long drive and parted ways at the cottage; he returned to his B&B and I took Jazz and immediately went to bed.

As exhausted as I was, sleep was elusive. I roamed around the dark cottage, looking out the windows at the police cars as they came and went to Rodney's estate. Jazz stayed by my side and I was glad he was with me.

Chapter Nineteen

I slept late the next morning until Jazz nudged me to let him out. I stumbled to the front door, unlocked it and he went out and around the corner. I walked into the kitchen and put the coffee together. As the coffee dripped into the glass carafe, I watched Jazz as he headed to the backyard. He saw me looking at him through the window and wagged his tail. I really missed my cat but I could see how dog owners could be captivated by their dog's affection and loyalty. He scratched at the back door and I opened it for him.

"Are your feet wet?" I asked, as he came into the kitchen, leaving wet paw prints all over the linoleum. "You answered my question," I commented as I got a piece of paper towel to wipe his paws and then the floor. "We have to take care of this place, Jazz, or your owner will be mad at us."

He looked around the room, hoping for breakfast. I rummaged around the cabinet shelves, refrigerator, and put together a meal that veterinarians wouldn't approve of. "I'll go shopping today and lunch will be better," I promised him as he gulped it down. I filled a large bowl with water and set it next to his food dish.

The phone rang and I went into the living room to answer it.

"Hello?" I said, expecting it to be Dan on the other end of the line.

"May, this is Amy Foster. Do you recall that we met at the market a couple of weeks ago? You offered to help with my bairns as we stood in the queue together."

"Of course, Amy. You asked me to come for tea." I remembered the young, harried mother of two who had told me the gossip about Steven Roberts, owner of the grocery, and Sarah, the young girl he'd gotten pregnant, and who now haunted the cottage.

"Yes, and that's why I'm calling. Could we meet in the next few days? I need to talk with you," she said, her voice shaky.

"I would enjoy seeing you again but is it something we could discuss over the phone?" I asked, wondering if childcare would be an issue for her.

"I'd rather we meet somewhere other than the village. I was thinking of that nice little restaurant right before you get to the turnoff for Stonehenge. Have you seen it?"

"Yes, I have. I'm curious, Amy, you sound so mysterious. Is anything wrong?" I asked, hearing her small children in the background.

"I just need to talk to you. My mum is taking care of my little terrors – would tomorrow afternoon be convenient, say about one o'clock? I could meet you there."

"Of course, I'll see you then."

I put the phone down. Whatever she had to tell me didn't sound like it was going to be pleasant. I had detected a tremor in her voice, almost like she was afraid of something. The restaurant was a definite tourist place. You couldn't miss it because the large tourist busses usually surrounded it. It would certainly be a place a local would stay away from, which is probably why she'd selected it.

I went back into the kitchen, poured a cup of fresh coffee and sat down at the scarred oak table to enjoy it. Jazz had found a spot of sunshine on the floor to lie in. It reminded me of my cat, Whiskers. She loved lying on a sunny windowsill. I wondered how she would react if I brought a dog home. I might look into it when I got back to Las Vegas.

After my coffee, I took a shower and got ready for the day. Amy's phone call kept popping up in my thoughts. Something wasn't right and I had no idea what it might be.

I locked the cottage, loaded Jazz into the Land Rover and off we went. It took about five minutes to drive to the grocery. I found a place to park right in front and was proud of myself for finally getting somewhat used to sitting in the right side of the car and driving on the left side of the road. I rolled the windows halfway down for Jazz but I wasn't worried about the heat. Clouds had covered the sun and rain was just beginning to fall as I walked into the store.

It took only a short while to gather up what I needed for Jazz and then I made my way to the front to pay. "No line," I commented to the older woman behind the register.

"Yes, it was hectic a little earlier but you timed it right, luv. Enjoying your stay, are you?" she asked as she scanned the items.

"It's been a busy time so far," I answered.

"According to the telly, there was some excitement out your way last evening. I was gobsmacked when I heard who'd been murdered at the manor house. Do they know who did it?" she asked as she put my few items into the small plastic-coated cotton bag I'd given her.

"I haven't heard anything," I said, as I paid her the amount listed on the computer screen.

"I'd be afraid to be out there. You be careful, luv. They'll catch whoever did it, just you see. Maybe you should think about moving into a nice B&B. My sister runs an excellent facility. Would you like me to call her for you?" she asked in a kind manner.

"No, ma'am, that won't be necessary. I feel safe where I am. But thanks for your concern."

"Well, if you change your mind, just let me know. Oh, in fact, I happen to have one of her little cards right next to the register. Here it is, all the info you'll need to contact her. She does run a clean, respectable business and I know you'd enjoy it," she said, giving me a pat on the hand along with the card.

I looked down at it and recognized the name. It was where Dan was staying. Fat chance I'd ever show up there, I thought as I went out to the car and loaded the bag into the trunk, or boot, as I'd been told was the correct name in these parts.

"Okay, Jazz, I'd thought about taking you with me, but I'm not. How does going home sound to you?" He wagged his tail so he must have liked the idea. Anyway, I thought I'd be nosy and find out what had taken place since last night.

I drove back to the cottage and turned onto the road that led to the manor house. As we emerged from the canopy of trees and saw the front of the house, it was evident things had quieted down. Only a few police cars remained and one vehicle that I thought must belong to the forensic team.

Driving around to the back on the little road that passed by the roses, it was hard to believe such violence had taken place just a few hours past. The lake sparkled in the distance and the wind had blown the rain clouds away. The sky was blue with those puffy white clouds that look as though they'd be a comfortable place to take a nap.

I stopped the car, let Jazz out and went in through the back entrance. The same officer I'd spoken to the evening before was still on duty. I hoped he'd had time to go home and get some rest. From his tired eyes and the dark shadow on the face, I would almost bet he'd been here the entire time.

"You look beat," I said, remembering the times I'd been in the exact same situation.

"I'm fine," he replied. "I see you've brought the dog back to us." He bent down and ruffled Jazz's ears and rubbed his fur. "I have a dog at home who looks a lot like this. Smart one, he is, too."

"Yes, he is that. I thought I'd leave him here while I go visit Rodney – Lord Willsdon – at the hospital in Swindon. I'll pick Jazz up later and take him back to the cottage with me."

"That should be fine. I'll make sure he's fed and watered," he said.

"Has any of the staff been around today?" I asked. Looking around, all I saw were police officers and those associated with them.

"No, we haven't seen any of the employees. I know we've been in contact with them, but so far, not one has shown up. They weren't here last night when we arrived, either."

"Even down at the stables? Someone must be taking care of the horses," I said.

He shook his head, "No, not that I've seen."

"Isn't that odd?" I asked, as I peered down the long hall that led to the front of the house.

"Yes, ma'am, quite odd."

"While I'm in Swindon with Lord Willsdon, I'll ask him what's going on."

"Actually, ma'am, that's been done already. Please excuse me, I must continue with my duties."

It was clear he was through talking with me at the moment. I thanked him and then walked down the hall toward the front of the house. When I got to the hidden door panel, on the right side of the hallway, I leaned down, slid back the bolt and opened it. Once on the other side, I closed it and slid the bolt back into place. It was a short hall, but there were four doors leading off of it. I opened the first one on my right and went inside. It was slightly larger than a closet and had stacks of paintings leaning against the wall. There were no windows and the light from the hall wasn't enough to illuminate the room. I looked where I thought a light switch should be, but couldn't find anything.

I went back into the hall, closed the door behind me and tried the next door. This room, also, had paintings and boxes, as though someone hadn't yet unpacked. There was a musty smell but that was to be expected with no windows to provide any ventilation.

The rooms on the other side of the hall were similar. I couldn't find the light switch in any of them. It made no sense. This house had been here for hundreds of years, yet here were four rooms with unpacked boxes of items. It made me wonder what the attic was used for. Isn't that where people usually put boxes and old paintings?

"Out of sight, out of mind," I said to myself. Maybe this was some sort of spring-cleaning. I would ask Rodney about this, too. He might wonder why I'd been snooping around his house, though.

I opened the door at the end of the hall without having to unlock it. I stepped out onto the small steps that led down to the drive that I'd used to get to the back of the house. The person who could have told me about the four rooms and unlocked side entry door had been murdered last night. Mrs. Long's body was autopsied by now, so any personal secrets she had were gone. At least the ones she could tell us about while she lived. Now, the secrets of her death would be taken from her in scientific and biological ways. I shivered as I thought about it. I'd never liked the part of detective work that involved visiting the morgue, although some of my colleagues in Las Vegas had taken a ghoulish interest in it.

I walked around to the car, got in and started the drive to Swindon to visit with Rodney. The ordered life that he had lived seemed to have fallen apart in the last few days. Of course, when you've lost your legs while serving in a war, life's obstacles take on a whole other meaning.

Chapter Twenty

"Hello, May," Rodney said as soon as I walked into his hospital room. "I thought you'd have been here earlier. And where's Jazz?"

"I left him at the manor house. I figured it might be easier for him to stay where he feels at home. I don't know anyone, human or animal, who likes hospital smells." I walked over and sat in a hard-backed chair that was next to his bed. "This chair is as uncomfortable as it looks, Rodney. Can't you snag something a little cushier than this?" I asked, as I scooted around trying to find a relaxed way to sit.

"If it's any consolation, May, this bed is awful, too," he replied, as he picked at the bedcovers. "I heard some terrible news about Mrs. Long. Have you any more information?"

"No, I don't, but they are working the cases non-stop. What a strange turn of events over the last few days, Rodney; first your solicitor, Mr. Reed was killed and now your long-time housekeeper. What in the world do you make of it?" I hoped I wasn't prying too much by asking these questions, because I knew DC Johnston had asked similar ones.

He looked at me with a puzzled expression and said, "I have no idea. I've been tossing and turning all night trying to make sense of it. It has to have something to do with those threatening letters I received, don't you think?"

"That would certainly be a path the police would follow, I'm sure. By the way, do you know why your staff has been staying away? When I left the estate this morning, even the stable workers hadn't shown up for work."

Rodney looked down at his hands as he continued to pick at a thread that was loose on his blanket. "It's something you wouldn't understand,

May. It has to do with our village life and 'the old ways,'" he said. "I'd like to ask one more favor of you, if you don't mind. Could you contact Leslie and ask her to do a cleansing? I'm afraid my staff won't come back until that's done."

I looked at him and thought he must be kidding. I'd heard of this, of course, but it usually involved the Navajo on their reservations in the Southwest. I didn't realize it was a part of English village life as well.

"Rodney, when you say 'cleansing' I'm thinking of a ceremony to get evil spirits to leave the area...is that correct?" I shifted in my uncomfortable wooden chair and wished for something softer.

"Yes, May, to send them back from whence they came. Our Leslie is the one to do that. I think you got a taste of her talents when you overheard the meeting in Lucy Davis' shoe shop." He looked at me and I noticed his left eyebrow was raised.

"How do you get your eyebrow to do that?" I asked. "And yes, I can request that Leslie do her magic work."

Rodney grinned, and it was good to see it. "I wasn't sure how you'd interpret our crazy little rituals. But then, that's why you American's cross the pond, isn't it, to come find the mysteries and magic of Stonehenge and the surrounds?"

I crossed my arms, sat back in the chair and said, "In my case, I came to England for peace and quiet. But as it turns out, Rodney, what I've fallen into is murder and confusion."

"Well, yes, I see what you mean. I'm sure things will go back to normal once Leslie gets on with her duties."

I was about to ask about the four small rooms filled with paintings and boxes when the nurse came rustling into the room, with a cursory nod in my direction. "And how is our star patient doing today?" she asked as she looked over charts and then peered into Rodney's eyes. "You look better, Lord Willsdon. You should be going home in a few days. I hear there was some sort of scrape last night involving you? You left the premises without permission?"

"Rodney," I interrupted, "how did you manage that?"

Before he could say a word, the starchy nurse had stuck a thermometer into his mouth. He raised his hands to indicate he couldn't answer.

"I'll leave you to the experts and on my way back to Maple Cottage

I'll stop and ask Leslie to 'work her magic.'"

I got up to leave, the nurse nodded to me, and she immediately started to close the semi-circular curtain around Rodney's bed. His fingers waggled to me as he disappeared behind the crisp whiteness of the curtain.

Closing the door behind me, I walked quickly down the glistening white corridor to the gleaming glass doors and out into the sunshine. I was always glad to get away from hospitals as fast as possible. Before getting into the Land Rover, I raised my face to the sun and appreciated the warmth on my skin. The hospital was in a beautiful location, surrounded by trees, grass and flowers. It looked like a park and I knew the patients and staff must enjoy being able to walk around it and rest on the many benches that were placed around the gardens. The red tulips, yellow daffodils and blue hyacinths looked especially riotous after the stark white of the hospital. I couldn't resist walking to the closest clump of pink roses and sticking my nose deep into the petals. Nothing smells better than this, I thought to myself. I stood there for a few moments longer, breathing in the fragrances around me. "Now this is England," I muttered out loud.

"Excuse me?" I heard a male voice say behind me.

I turned and looked up into the chocolate-brown eyes of a man who was dressed in a kilt with a bagpipe over his shoulder. I didn't recognize the clan colors he was wearing but it really didn't matter.

"I don't mean to intrude," his lilting Scottish voice informed me, "but I thought you might need assistance. Can I be of service?" he asked

What was going through my mind and what I said had nothing in common with each other. "Just enjoying the beauty of the garden. I'll be on my way now," I said, heading toward the car, hoping he would run after me and whisk me off to the Highlands.

I got into the car and sat for a few moments, watching as he began to walk around the garden playing the bagpipes. I didn't recognize the tune but I was sure it was a welcome sound for those incarcerated inside the hospital walls.

The drive returning to the village took longer because the tour busses were out in force. When I got to the restaurant near Stonehenge I looked up at the curving road that led to it. I almost turned onto the drive to go up and have a look, but remembered I needed to tell Leslie about

Rodney's request. Anyway, I'd be back tomorrow to meet with Amy Foster.

By the time I turned into the car park at the Prince and Pauper, I was ready for one of Leslie's terrific meals. I parked the car; surprised I found an open place, got out and locked the doors with the use of the key fob. Inside, as usual, it was packed. Leslie saw me right away and came over.

"How good to see you, May. Come in for a bite to eat? From the looks of you, you miss too many meals. If you were searching for your man, he just left. In fact, he was asking for you," she said, as she waved me to follow her to a small table near a mullioned window.

"My man?" I asked, as I took a seat at a square oak table that had a small pot of fresh flowers on top.

She looked at me, cocking her head to the left. "Yes, May, the man who cares for you more than you want to admit."

"If he's tall and Scottish, I'm interested," I replied.

Leslie laughed and so did I. Then I asked if she could sit with me for a few minutes. "I have a message for you from Rodney," I told her as she pulled up the chair and joined me.

"Oh?" she asked, twirling a long lock of blonde hair around her blood-red manicured fingernails.

"He asked that you do 'the cleansing spell' at the manor house to get rid of the evil spirits. It seems the staff won't return to work until you've done this. And while I'm on the topic, I think I heard you invoking 'spirits' when I was snooping around the shoe shop one afternoon. What's that about?"

"Our customs must seem strange to you, May," she said. "I heard you were in the shop that day. Those rituals are left over from my mum's time and a few still follow them. It's harmless. As for the cleansing at the manor house, I finished it. Went over before I opened the pub this morning. Everything is fine; all of the staff is back at work, to include in the stables. That's the part that worried you, wasn't it, that the horses needed to be fed?" she asked, a little smile playing around the corners of her bee-stung red lips. "You worry about dogs and horses and people getting fed and taken care of, but you never feed yourself properly, food or love. Why do you run away from it, May? Have you been so hurt in your life that it scares you? I know your husband, Dan, made some terrible choices, but he regrets it. He does care for you, May, even more than the money you have." She patted my hands, which were laying on the tabletop. "I'm going back to the kitchen and get you the biggest piece of steak I can find. You need protein. That will put the color back in your cheeks."

She got up from the chair, took a couple of steps then turned back to me and said, "Oh, yes, about the Scottish gentlemen. He'll be in your life sooner than you think. Now whether or not you'll let him stay there, that's another thing."

I was so surprised by what she'd said I just sat there, watching as she sashayed her curvy body around the close-packed tables and disappeared into the kitchen area of the pub.

Within fifteen minutes I had a huge slab of prime rib in front of me, a baked potato covered with butter, sour cream and what looked like cheese. "Is there anything else you could have found in the kitchen that would make this meal more fattening?" I asked Leslie, as I dove into it.

"Now that you mention it, I forgot the rolls. I'll be back."

Upon her return, I had yeast rolls, butter and a large glass of milk added to the menu. "I don't really need to gain weight," I said, gulping down the food.

"Yes, you do. Your body is screaming to be fed."

I paused to take a drink of the cold milk, and then asked again about Leslie's mother. "I keep hearing comments about 'the old ways.' What's that about?"

Leslie watched as I tackled the food again. "It was a way of life that existed here for time out of mind. My mum would be considered a witch in some circles, a goddess in others, but she did more good than bad. But I can't tell you that she didn't cause great harm. I've tried to be judicious in what I do with my powers," she said, watching me closely.

I stopped eating, wiped my mouth with the linen napkin, and asked, "Did you just tell me you're a witch-goddess?"

"In the best possible sense of the words," she answered.

Chapter Twenty-One

The Stonehenge Restaurant was crowded. I had arrived early on purpose so I could get a quiet table. As I looked around I realized that wouldn't be possible. It was a cacophony of noise, hustle and bustle. My second choice was a table with a view and that was easier to provide for the harried woman who led me to a table. I realized after I sat down that this was the best view of Stonehenge I'd ever seen. Because the restaurant was on a hill, Stonehenge and the Salisbury Plain were in direct sight; even the bus and car park was out of range around the curve of the road. People wandered outside the barriers that had been erected to protect the stones a few years ago. The fences, however, didn't take away from the overpowering sense of the place. I was so engrossed in the view that I jumped when Amy said, "Hello, May, and thanks for coming." She, too, had arrived early.

We made our polite comments, a waiter came over to take our order, I folded my hands on the table and asked, "What's wrong, Amy? Why are you so nervous?"

Amy looked even younger in the harsh light. Her eyes were puffy and she kept looking anywhere else except at me. "I shouldn't be telling you this," she finally said, "but I didn't know whom else to talk to."

Considering I'd met this young woman once in a grocery store I was surprised by the comment. Many people in Las Vegas, and DC Johnston, had told me that the English were standoffish, especially with foreigners. So far, none of that had been true.

"Why me, Amy? I don't really know you and you certainly don't know me."

"But that's just it. You're not a part of it. And you're an American and that means you're not bogged down in all these awful legends and spells and things." Amy looked at me, finally, and fat tears rolled down her cheeks. "I'm afraid for my baby, May. I'm scared they'll take my baby."

Hairs stood up on the back of my neck. I had a sense that Sarah, the ghost of Maple Cottage, was with us. This time, I couldn't look at Amy. This was too much. I was still agog over what Leslie had told me yesterday in her pub.

"You have to forgive me, Amy, I'm having trouble processing this information." I took a deep breath, and as my dear friend Detective Harvey Jordan had taught me long ago, I continued the discussion, no matter what I thought about things. "Can you tell me who it is you're afraid of, Amy? Does your husband know about this?"

"I know it sounds like rubbish to your ears, May, but it's what we live with around here. The whole place is nothing but spells and crazy things that can make people die, and take babies from mothers bodies...." Tears streaked down her face and she shook her head to indicate she couldn't continue.

With that, she got up and left, I presumed to go to the restroom to regain control of her emotions. However, after a few minutes, I had the feeling she'd gone. I got up and went in search of her, but was told that she'd run out of the restaurant and had been sobbing.

I went outside and looked around the car park, but knew her car wouldn't be there. I felt terrible. So much for my investigative skills, I thought, as I went back in to pay the bill.

When I got back to my car, I pulled my cell phone out of my purse. Digging around the bottom of my bag, I found DC Johnston's card and punched in the numbers. Surprisingly, he answered.

I told him about my sad and very brief meeting with Amy Foster. Before he could say much, he informed me there had been an accident on the highway, not far from where I was, and he had to ring off immediately.

No, I told myself, it can't be Amy. I started the Land Rover and drove down the hill, turning right onto the busy highway. I had to concentrate to make sure I went into the correct lane. I was upset with the meeting and scared that Amy had come to a bad end.

I didn't have to go far to find the wreck. Smoke billowed from the bottom of the car, which was turned upside down in a ditch. The fire trucks were screaming their way to the scene, from Swindon, I presumed, and I quickly pulled into a lay by so they could pass. Police cars were already there and I knew DC Johnston was on his way. What I didn't know was who was driving the car. I opened my car door and gingerly stepped down from the high seat. I was reluctant to intrude but felt compelled to walk toward the scene. The firemen were shouting at each other and pulling hoses from the two trucks. At that moment, the car exploded and lit the sky with bright orange-yellow light and black smoke. The heat forced me back and I stumbled as I retreated closer to my car. I marveled at the firemen, who in the flames and heat and danger, continued to move forward.

More police cars had arrived and I saw that DC Johnston was with them. He went up to the fireman who was manning the pumps at the truck and they spoke. The detective looked around and I waved at him. He walked in my direction.

"There's someone in the vehicle. The firemen saw her when they first went near it," he said to me as he continued to watch the flames as the firemen heroically tried to get them under control. "I was hoping whoever was in there would have been thrown clear," he said.

"Is it Amy Foster?" I asked.

"We're checking the car registration now. Do you know what type of car she was driving, May?"

"No, I never saw it," I replied.

There was a secondary explosion and one of the firemen was blown back from the force of it. I turned my head because I couldn't watch anymore. What I saw in the other direction was Stonehenge, still powerful after a thousand years.

* * *

The fire was contained and the injured fireman was taken away by ambulance to the same hospital as Rodney.

DC Johnston had walked partway to the scene when one of the firemen approached him. Both of them turned and walked toward me.

"May," the detective said when they reached me; "the car was registered to Amy Foster's husband, so we are presuming it must be her inside. Unfortunately, the body has been burned beyond recognition. It will have to be the coroner who confirms identity. I'm sorry," he said, and put his hand on my shoulder.

I felt sick and covered my mouth with my hand. The firemen pulled off his helmet and facemask. I looked into the chocolate-brown eyes of the Scottish bagpiper.

"Can I be of service?" he asked in his lilting voice.

"That's the second time you've asked me that in two days," I answered.

DC Johnston looked from one to the other and asked, "You two know each other?"

"No," we replied in unison.

The detective pulled on his ear and said, "Hmm, yes, I'm going back to the scene now. You two, um, carry on."

We watched him leave and, embarrassed, turned toward each other.

"My name is May Scott, tourist from Las Vegas, glad to meet you," I said, looking at my feet.

"My name is Hamish Campbell, firefighter from Aberdeen, Scotland, glad to meet you."

When I looked up, I saw he had a very big smile on his face. "Are we legal now?" he asked.

I began to back up and said, "Well, I need to go now. Nice to meet you and good-bye." I felt like I was in junior high and knew I was blushing.

"You can't leave yet," he said, still grinning.

"I have to," I said, trying not to notice the dimple in his chin.

"The road is blocked, Miss. Look at the back-up." He pointed out to me that the road was jammed in both directions.

"Um, okay, I'll go sit in my car." I turned to walk to the Land Rover, which was about ten feet away.

"Ta, ta, Miss," he said to my retreating back.

I got in the car and felt dumb. Then I wondered what he was doing fighting a fire in England when he said he was from Aberdeen, Scotland. "This whole place is nuts," I decided. But I watched every step he took as he walked away from me.

Chapter Twenty-Two

By the time I got back to Maple Cottage, it was early evening. I unlocked the door to the cottage and went immediately into the bathroom to take a long, hot shower. I washed my hair and did all sorts of grooming that I hadn't done in a while. At the back of my mind, I knew I was hoping I'd get a call from Hamish. I finally understood what the term "gobsmacked" meant.

After I got out of the shower and put on clean clothes, I took a small load of laundry into the kitchen to wash them. This was the second time I'd used the washer and it was hard to operate. I rolled it over to the sink and hooked up the hoses to the hot and cold-water faucets. It was as if everything about it was backwards from what I was used to. To include, it was tiny. The first time I'd used it I hung the clothes out to dry on the line in the backyard. This time, I'd have to figure out how the dryer operated. I looked at it briefly, hoped I had it figured out, and then headed for the refrigerator. I had just made myself a huge ham and cheese sandwich when the phone rang.

I ran into the living room, trying to catch my breath and stop my heart from pounding. I picked up the receiver, knowing I'd hear that lovely voice again.

"Hello?" I answered in my most seductive tones.

"Where in the hell have you been? I must have called you a dozen times and I even stopped by that armpit of a place you're staying. Didn't you get my messages? And I know Leslie told you I'd come by her place looking for you."

I held the receiver away from my ear then gently put it back in the cradle. I returned to the kitchen and ate my sandwich, followed by a few handfuls of cookies and a big glass of milk. I'd decided I wanted to have a curvy figure like Leslie. Being a walking bag of bones wasn't conducive to romance.

As I suspected, Dan didn't give up. When I saw the headlights turn into the cottage driveway, I knew who it was. I watched him get out of his car and walk to the door, which I had opened for him.

"What's wrong with you, Eva May? You at least used to be polite. You can't take two minutes to talk to me when I call you?" He had his hands on his hips and he looked self-righteous.

"I'd offer you coffee but I'm using the kitchen sink to wash clothes. Of course, I could use the tap in the bathroom if you really want a cup. Oh, and please do come in. Have a seat." I waved toward the couch.

"Are you on drugs? I always thought you needed some sort of anti-depressant or whatever that passive-aggressive thing is." He sat down and looked at me for a few long moments. "What's that goofy look on your face? Have you met someone?"

"No," I lied. "When are you leaving? I'll buy your ticket. Even take you to the airport."

Before he could reply, the phone rang again and I smiled. I lunged for it and did my seductive voice again. This time it was DC Johnston. Hearing his voice brought me back to reality about what had occurred today. As much as I wanted to block it from my mind, by whatever means available, it was now conclusive. The body belonged to Amy Foster. He was coming to talk to me and I knew I had to stop this silly daydreaming. When I hung up the phone, the old me was back. No more curvy body and romance, just murder and mayhem.

"DC Johnston is coming over, Dan. You have to leave. I did get your messages but, and let me make this very clear to you. I don't want you in my life; I can't stand you; go away and stop stalking me. You have a young wife and two precious children. Go home to them and stop this nonsense about me. It will never happen, Dan. Is that clear enough?" I asked.

"You've met someone. Who is it, that detective? I always thought there was something going on with you two. I'll beat him within an inch of his life, and it doesn't matter he's twice my size." He stood up, all five feet five inches of him, and started punching the air with his small fists.

I tried not to laugh, but he looked funny. It was just a little giggle but he heard it. "That's it, May, I'm out of here. You'll never see me again," he stormed as he headed for the door, which I had opened for him. When he went through it, I closed and locked it, then pulled the curtains. I could tell he'd left because his tires screeched as he tore out of the driveway.

I had put the clothes in the dryer and tidied the kitchen when DC Johnston arrived. By the time he was in the cottage and sitting down, the coffeepot beeped that it was ready. I got us both a cup of fresh coffee and we started the conversation.

I told him everything I knew about Amy, as brief as it was, especially the painful time we'd spent in the restaurant earlier in the day.

"My impression, from the phone call, and then in person, was that she was terrified. At first I'd thought it was nerves, but the girl was scared. And in retrospect, she had a right to be. Was she murdered?" I asked as I took a sip of coffee.

"The FET is looking into that now," he replied.

"Excuse me? FET? What's that?" I asked.

"Oh, sorry. It means Fire Examination Team. They are called up when anything isn't looking quite proper."

"The explosions, both of them, were excessively violent and intensely hot. Much more so than, dare I say this, your run-of-the-mill type. I thought it was a bomb or several of them. It was much more violent than when Rodney's Suburban was blown up. And her car was so much smaller than his," I said then took a sip of coffee.

"Yes, I thought of that straight away," he replied. "We should know something soon, they're still working the site. I wanted to mention that Lord Willsdon's dog is being cared for by staff, so you're relieved of that duty. By the way, what's this between you and Campbell, if I may ask?"

I rubbed my eyes and wanted to be left alone. "I saw him at the hospital, after I'd visited Rodney. He plays the bagpipes; I suppose to entertain the patients. I always thought bagpipes sounded like screeching cats, but somehow his sounded better."

DC Johnston looked at me for a few moments longer than was necessary, then said, "He asked about you."

I couldn't help it. I smiled.

He saw it and understood what it meant. "Well, I'd say he's a lucky man."

"I don't think my ex-husband would agree. He just left in a big huff. If I'm lucky, he'll never speak to me again. By the way, whatever happened to those bones that were found in the woods? I kept meaning to ask you about them, but so many other things have taken over," I said, glad to be off the topic of Hamish Campbell.

He put his cup down and sat back more comfortably in the couch cushions. "They are, of course, being looked at. We sent them to Scotland Yard. That may take a while. So far, we have our suspicions, but won't know for sure until we get the report back."

"Does it have anything to do with any of the other open cases?" I asked, even though it wasn't any of my business.

"Possible but not certain. Anyway, I thought you were retired from this sort of thing," he said, grinning.

"I remember how disgusted I used to get when detectives retired, then the next week they were in our offices sitting around wasting our time. It's like a big club that you never really leave, don't you think?"

"Don't know yet. My time is down the road a ways. I do get the bit about the retirees coming back in to visit. Happens all the time. Sometimes they can be a bother, but more often than not, they've been a big help to me," he replied.

His comments made me feel guilty. "I hope I haven't been too much of a bother to your investigations."

DC Johnston looked at me and said, "It's been a pleasure, actually. You look at things in a different way, that's all."

He left in a few minutes and I closed and locked the door behind him. After Rodney came home from the hospital, I wondered it was time for me to leave. I'd had enough of a vacation, such as it was.

I pulled my clothes from the dryer and draped them around the kitchen chairs to completely dry. I could guess what Leslie would say when she heard I was thinking about leaving – that I was, once again, running away.

Chapter Twenty-Three

I slept better than I had for a while and when I pulled the curtains back, the day was sunny and glorious. I quickly put on my clothes and went outside to walk along the river that was across the road from Maple Cottage. A yellowish-stone bridge led to a trail on the other side of the waterway.

I had meant to take Jazz for a walk along the footpath that followed the curves of the water, but never got around to it. Sometime today, I'd take the dog food over that I'd bought for him yesterday. When DC Johnston told me Jazz would be taken care of by Rodney's staff, I had been sorry to hear it.

I did my best not to think about Amy, Sarah, Rodney, Mrs. Long, and Michael Reed. After awhile, it actually worked. I sat on a bench and watched as the narrow boats drifted by. Some had tourists on board and they waved to me as they meandered down the river. I could smell the overturned earth that the farmers were readying for their crops. The green-leafed trees and the purple-and-white wildflowers dazzled and the water sparkled. Birds twittered in the huge elms, some with such long branches that they floated on top of the water. I was startled by the ring-ring tones of a bicycle bell that made me look around. I waved to the woman who rode by, her basket filled with purchases from the village.

"Think I'll stay for a little while longer," I said to the sparrows that sat at my feet, waiting for a handout. I got up from the bench and they rose up into the air, finally getting the message that I had no crumbs to give them. I watched as they flew over to the fields, and settled down to try their luck with any bugs or worms that might have been turned up in the soil by the farmer's plow. I turned to start the short walk back to the cottage when I heard a voice call my name.

"Miss Scott? Could I have a moment, please?" the woman on the bicycle asked as she got off the bike and pushed it toward me.

I didn't recognize her but I could tell she was upset. She was middle-aged, plump and her limp brown hair fell around her round face in an unattractive manner. Her eyes welled with tears and she wiped them away as she approached me. "I'm Amy Foster's mum, Doris Owen. We saw you one day in the village and she pointed you out to me. She said she liked you right away, that you were easy to talk to."

What could I say to this woman? I was so stunned that I was mute. Finally I asked if she would like to sit down on the bench.

She did, propping the bike against the back of it. I joined her. "I am so dreadfully sorry for your loss," I began and then stopped.

Mrs. Owen said "I know there are no words – for anybody. It was a terrible accident. Her husband, Bruce, feels like it's his fault because he talked her into that hybrid car. She wanted a big SUV for the young ones. He says he can never work on another car as long as he lives. He's a mechanic in my husband's garage." Tears continued to stream down her face and she pulled tissues out of her pocket and blew her nose. "She told me she was going to talk to you. Did you get to speak to Amy?" she asked.

How could I tell this poor grieving mother that her daughter had left the restaurant before telling me anything? Her trip had been unnecessary, and if she hadn't driven out there, she'd be alive today. Tears streamed down my face and words wouldn't come. She handed me a tissue and we both sat there in silence.

After a few minutes I wiped my eyes, took a deep breath and said, "I spoke with Amy for a few minutes but she never told me what it was she was so upset about. In fact, she left the restaurant and I didn't know it. I found out when I went searching for her, because she'd been gone so long."

"I know what she wanted to tell you," Mrs. Owen said. "Somebody had been sending her threatening letters, telling her she was to be the next village 'heroine.'"

"Village heroine?" That term sounded familiar. "Isn't that what they call Sarah Demming?"

Mrs. Owen looked at me, wiped her eyes again, and said, "Yes, exactly. That's why it scared Amy so. She knew what had happened to Sarah."

I felt the hairs on my neck standing up. "Was Sarah murdered?"

Mrs. Own took my hand in hers. "I see now why Amy wanted to talk to you. You piece things together, don't you? My Amy died in a tragic car accident. I only heard about the letters, never got to read them myself. I was hoping Amy had given them to you."

"No, she didn't."

Mrs. Owen patted my hand and stood up. "I have to go. I've been searching for those letters and if I find them, you'll be the one I give them to."

She pushed her bike a little ways, got on and rode down the path.

I knew where the letters were. They'd gone up in flames with Amy in that terrible fire. I walked back toward the bridge, crossed over, and returned to the cottage.

* * *

As I sat in the kitchen with my filled coffee cup, the phone jangled me out of my stupor. After the last few days, I was almost afraid to answer it. Of course, it might be that Scottish fireman calling, I thought to myself as I went into the living room to answer.

"Hello, May?" a discombobulated voice said.

"Yes, this is she. Who is this, please?"

"If you don't leave immediately, you'll die," the voice said.

I heard the line click and I sighed. I knew I shouldn't have answered that call.

It didn't take long for DC Johnston to arrive, forensics team in tow. Before we got to the call I had received, I told him about my talk with Mrs. Owen. He said he would contact her as soon as possible.

"Why," I asked him, "do you need so many people to trace a phone call? Can't you do that from the station?"

"Well, yes and no. These telephone devices are so old that we need special equipment to deal with them. And you have no idea who this caller was, man or woman?" he asked as he sat on the couch, writing in

135

his moleskin notebook.

"None," I said, noting that he was dressed very nicely today. "Are you going to a wedding or some other such occasion?" I asked, clearly being nosy.

"Hum, what?" he asked, focused on his writing tasks.

"Never mind," I replied, wondering what Hamish Campbell was doing. Why hadn't he called me yet, I wondered, thank goodness not out loud.

"I want you to move out of here, May. In fact, it might very well be in your best welfare to leave the area. If we need further information, we can always do a conference call to you in Las Vegas," he said, closing his notebook.

"How do you know I'm not a suspect?"

He sat back and observed me for a moment. "Are you?" he countered.

"That's for you to find out, isn't it? Anyway, I'm not going anywhere for the time being. I'll be okay here. I can take care of myself," I said, meaning every word.

"Yes, I'm sure that's true. And I'll bet each of our victims thought the same thing. The other alternative is, I'll have someone move in with you."

My mind leaped to all sorts of tempting possibilities.

But what he came up with was, "How about that ex-husband of yours. Would that work for a few days?"

"I'd rather live with Jack the Ripper. Is he available?"

"All right. Bad suggestion. We're so short-handed at the moment, it's hard to pull an officer from the team to stay here; but that's not your problem. I'll have someone here before nightfall. Are you going to be in this evening?" he asked, standing up to leave.

"Yes, I should be here. I need to walk over to the manor house and leave some food I bought for Jazz. Then I'll come right back," I promised.

"Keep your doors locked. The telephone line is hooked into ours so any calls you receive will be monitored." That was his parting comment as he waved and left with the additional officers.

After their cars had driven away, I went into the backyard and sat down on one of the garden chairs that were arranged around the small patio. The day was so beautiful and I'd had such a lovely time on my walk earlier in the morning. It was one of the few times I'd really enjoyed being in the English countryside. Maybe DC Johnston and Dan were right; perhaps I should pack up and leave before something else happened.

The phone rang and I walked back into the cottage to answer.

"Hello?" I said, knowing that people were listening.

"Miss Scott? This is Hamish Campbell. I would like to invite you to have dinner with me this evening," he said, in his thick Scottish brogue.

All thoughts of leaving left my mind. "I'd be delighted. What time and where?" I asked, wondering what in the world I had to wear.

As soon as I hung up the phone, I gathered Jazz's food and prepared to take it to the manor house. I made sure to lock the back door securely on my way out. It took about half an hour to drop the food off and return to the cottage.

I was thinking about making a short foray into the village to look for a new dress. As I approached the cottage I noticed that the dilapidated garden shed had a light shining through the cobwebbed windows. I walked over to peer inside but couldn't see much because of the dirty windows. Walking around to the door, which was closed, I turned the handle and pushed it open. I took a tentative step inside and was shoved from behind so violently that I fell forward onto the wooden floor.

I turned my head and pushed myself up just as the door was pulled shut and locked. Hearing a noise that sounded eerily familiar, I looked in that direction and stared straight into the hooded eyes of the biggest rattlesnake I had ever seen, at least that close.

The snake was coiled into the familiar striking pose and his brownish tan scales, designed for the desert, didn't conceal him on the dark wood of the floor. I'd attended classes several times during my years as a police office on how to deal with snakes and their bite so I was somewhat knowledgeable of how to react. I turned into stone, not moving, not even blinking. My breathing slowed and I went into what I thought of as my yoga pose for survival.

It seemed like hours until the snake uncoiled and slithered off to the back reaches of the shed. I stayed where I was for a few minutes because I knew the rattler was watching. Listening to any sounds around me, I slowly stood up and backed toward the door, which I knew was locked.

It gave me a chance, though, to look around the shed.

My hands behind my back, I tried the door handle anyway. There would be no easy exit there so I moved to a window. Still with my body toward where I thought the snake was hiding, I turned sideways and tried to open the window. It was immovable as well.

A burlap bag lay on the floor, and I leaned over slowly to pick it up. Covering my left hand with it, I pushed on the glass in the window and it gave easily. Having success made me less cautious, and I moved an old chair over to the window to stand on while I pushed out the rest of the glass. When I'd made sure no jagged edges remained, I crawled through the opening and jumped the short distance to the ground. Running toward the cottage, I imagined the snake was hot on my trail.

I got the back door open and quickly closed it behind me. I stood there for a few moments, hoping my breath would get back to normal. Splashing water onto my face seemed like a good idea, so I went into the small bathroom and leaned over the sink. The cold water felt good and I reached for the hand towel to dry my face.

As I stood in front of the mirror, Sarah's face appeared and her mouth was moving but I couldn't hear her words. Then she vanished and I was left to wonder what she so obviously wanted to tell me.

Before I called DC Johnston, I sat in the living room and thought about what I should do. I had forgotten about my dinner date. Anyway, I'd lost all interest.

Chapter Twenty-Four

By the time DC Johnston and crew returned, I had packed and was ready to move on. I hadn't quite decided where I'd land, but my days at this cottage had ended. I showed the police officers and forensics techs where I'd last seen the snake. "Just to clarify, where would a snake from the southwest U.S. desert come from around here?" I asked to anyone who wanted to answer.

"We have a zoo in Swindon and it has a reptile display," a young man answered, covered from head to foot in a scene of crime outfit.

"And they have rattlesnakes from the desert southwest. So who ever put the snake in the garden shed has access to the zoo. I think he or she used the burlap bag to transport the snake," I said. "It came in handy to break the windows with, too, so inadvertently, they helped me escape."

DC Johnston added, "Agreed. Now, let's get you out of here."

"I'm ready. Any suggestions as to where I should go?"

"Home with me," he replied.

I turned and looked at him. "What did you say?" I asked, confused. "I don't think I understood what you said. Did you say stay at your house? What are you thinking?"

"It makes perfect sense. Let's go get your bags and I'll take you home."

We walked toward the cottage and before we got to the back door I told him I couldn't go to his house. "I'll check into the B&B where my ex is staying."

"They're filled, I think. No room at the inn. Anyway, I discussed it with my boss and she said it would be proper for you to stay with me."

"I'm glad you and your boss agree. It's me who's not so crazy about

139

it," I replied.

By this time we'd gone inside and I had gathered up my bags. He helped me move them into the living room. I unlocked the front door and we carried them outside to my rental car.

"I don't want you to think I don't appreciate your offer, it's just not something I feel comfortable in doing." I tried to be polite but this man was pushing my buttons.

DC Johnston sighed, and then nodded in agreement. "Let me know where you are. I'll keep it close. My suggestion is that you get on the next flight out of Heathrow."

"I just may do that," I said, opening the back of the Land Rover and shoving my bags inside.

"You travel light," he commented as he pushed the bags further back into the boot, then closed the door.

I held out my hand, "Thank you for all you've done to help me. I know you'll get this case solved. Keep me in the loop, please."

He covered my hand with both of his and told me he would.

I opened the car door, and then remembered I still had the cottage key. "Could you give this to Rodney?" I asked, as I handed it to him.

"Of course," he replied. He then turned and walked back toward the garden shed.

I got into the car, started it and wheeled onto the road. I wasn't sad to be leaving. Now, where was I going?

I got as far as the "Prince and Pauper" and turned into the parking lot. Maybe Leslie could help me with some of the questions I had.

* * *

By the time I had gone inside, had something to eat and was scraping the plate that had held a piece of the best chocolate cake I'd ever eaten, Leslie came and joined me. "Do you want another slice of cake? It would do you good," she said.

"You know, I do. And could I have another scoop of vanilla ice cream on top?" In for a penny, in for a pound, I thought, as I unbuttoned the top of my pants.

While I waited, I pulled out my cell phone and called Hamish

Campbell's number. As I expected, I had to leave a message, which I did. I felt relieved I didn't have to see him again. I didn't want any more complications, and I knew he would be.

Leslie returned from her glorious kitchen laden with another slice of heaven. I groaned my way through it while she laughed at me.

"You are a delightful crazy person," she said.

"Right back at you, Dolly," I countered. I'd already told her she reminded me of the American singer.

"Now, what's happened that you're in here eating like a lorry driver," she asked, chin resting in her palm.

I told her everything; about the ghost, Amy, Mrs. Owen, the snake and DC Johnston's offer of a place to stay.

"I wish I could understand what Sarah is saying. I think if I knew that, I'd solve all of this. She's the key."

Leslie looked thoughtful and took her time before she answered. "I agree. Sarah is trying to tell us something. Has been for years. You're not the first, you know, to see her."

"You were just a child when all of this was going on. Do you remember anything about it?" I asked, as I leaned back in the chair.

"I recall everything – at least the parts I got to see. My mother sent me to visit friends when things got too scary. Of course, with her, sometimes she was more frightening than anything else." Leslie put her hands on top of the table and leaned forward. "I loved my mother, but when I was little, I used to dream of having a 'normal' mum like everyone else. As for you, I have one solution. Move in with me."

I grinned and said, "I'd love to. Where do you call home?"

"You'll be surprised," she said. "Let me go tell them I'll be gone for a while and I'll take you there." She got up and headed for the kitchen.

This felt better. I could stay with Leslie and we could have a pajama party and roast marshmallows. It would be normal and quiet and no one would get killed or have snakes crawling around. I wondered how long I'd be having nightmares about those hooded eyes on that big rattlesnake. I hope they'd caught the snake and returned him to the Swindon zoo.

Leslie came back and I followed her out to the parking lot.

"I'll drive slow so you can keep up with me," she said as she headed for her yellow sports car.

I climbed into the Land Rover and prepared to follow Leslie as she led me to her home.

We turned toward the village and before she got to the High Street, she made a sharp left turn onto a narrow road that wasn't much larger than a path. I hoped we didn't meet another car because I had no idea what to do if that happened. We drove deeper into the woods and I pushed a button to make the driver-side window go down. The air was still and the woods were silent except for the noise our tires made as they crunched along the rough ground.

We came to a clearing and there sat a whitewashed stone cottage with a thatched roof made from reeds and straw. It was in a lovely open space that allowed the sun in, and was not far from the bustle of the village.

Leslie got out of her car and motioned for me to continue to follow her, this time on foot. I opened the car door and got out. A big black cat sat at the front door, waiting to go inside. A huge purple wisteria had formed an arch over the entryway so we walked under fragrant, purple flowers to the front door.

"This is Mouser. I hope you like cats," Leslie said as she opened the unlocked door.

"I love cats. My cat's name is Whiskers and she saved my life not long ago."

Leslie turned to me and said, "My, what an interesting life you've had, May. I want to hear about that chapter. Please, come inside and make yourself very much at home."

I walked into the cottage and it was the most beautiful room I'd ever seen. The large river rock stone fireplace had a huge copper pot filled with red geraniums placed where logs would go in the cold months. Couches and chairs covered in shades of white and cream nestled in various arrangements around the room. It wasn't a great-sized space but the way Leslie had it arranged made it seem so. Sheer curtained windows let the light in and cushions on the large sills would be a wonderful place to read a book or nap.

"This is fantastic, Leslie. Did you do this yourself? If so, you should be a decorator."

"This is my mother's house. It's pretty much as she left it, although I have re-done the fabric on the furniture and the curtains. It's much as I recall from my childhood."

"Your husband lived here with you?" I asked, knowing this was none of my business.

"Yes. At first he didn't like it but it grew on him." She moved into another room and called me in. "This will be your bedroom and sitting area. There's a bath right over there," she pointed to an opened door. "I want you to stay here and enjoy yourself as long as you like. You can look around and help yourself to anything in the kitchen. It's a pleasure to have you with me. I'm too much alone."

"I will become one with my environment," I said. "And thank you for making me feel so welcome."

"Good, so now I'm off for work. I'll be in late tonight. If you want to lock yourself in, not to worry, I have a key with me."

"I wondered about that," I said, continuing to take in the beautiful bedroom. "Was this your room when you were a little girl?" I asked.

"Oh, yes. I loved this room. In fact, I may move back in here one day soon."

With that, she left, waving a quick good-bye.

I looked around the bedroom and was enclosed in solidity and warmth. The towels in the elegant bath were sheet-sized and sparkling white and the tub had claw feet and looked very inviting. I made a quick decision to get my bags from the car, and then take a nice soak in the tub.

Mouser watched me from the door and I petted him on my way out. He was much larger than Whiskers, who weighted only ten pounds. He was at least twice her size. I hoped he approved of my visit. So far, he seemed to.

After I had hauled my luggage inside, I went back out into the sunshine and walked around the small house. Even though we couldn't be too far from the village, I didn't hear traffic noise or anything else that would lead one to believe there was a bustling community somewhere behind the trees. The house looked in pristine condition even though I knew it must be over a hundred years old. I would have to ask Leslie who did her gardens because they rivaled any I'd seen in public parks.

When I went back inside I took a few minutes to roam around and look at old photos that were sitting on the antique furniture and the

143

fireplace mantel. There were several of Leslie and her mother, Mrs. Long, and one of Steven Roberts. I was surprised to see his photo and picked it up to take a closer look. There was still a glimmer of the slender young man in the current Mr. Roberts. It still eluded me why Sarah had been so enamored of him. But then, look at Dan. What had I been thinking? Another photo got my attention. It was a Christmas card of Lord and Lady Willsdon and Rodney when he was about twelve years old, possibly older. He stood a little apart from them, and with his dark coloring and facial features, didn't resemble them at all.

Leslie's home looked like it was used lovingly and cared for, but not turned into a "don't touch anything" museum. There was a comforting quality about the place, like a sanctuary, where you felt welcomed and safe.

The kitchen was old but efficient. The appliances looked to be from the fifties and they sparkled. I took a cup down from a cabinet that had glass panes instead of solid doors. You could see all the colored dishware, canned goods and spices. It was not only colorful but also useful because you didn't have to rummage around looking for things.

I turned on the tap and filled the cup with cool water. It was so good I had two more cups before I took myself off to the bath for a long soak.

In fact, I was so comfortable in the deep tub I fell asleep. When I woke the water had cooled, so I added a little more hot water and continued to soak.

When I got out of the tub, I dried off, pulled on my pajamas and lay down on the soft bed for just a little while. The next time I woke, it was seven the next morning and I felt wonderful. I stretched, got out of bed and walked over to the window to look out. There had been heavy dew and the grass and flowers were covered with droplets of water that sparkled like silver in the sunshine.

"This must be what heaven is like," I said out loud.

"Why, thank you! In that case, that makes me an angel delivering your morning coffee, I guess," Leslie said as she brought a tray into the room. "I hope you don't mind my barging in, but I heard you get up."

"Perfect timing and it smells wonderful," I said as I reached for the cup of coffee that Leslie offered me.

"I gather you slept well?"

"Better than I have in months. I haven't felt this good since before my friend Harvey and his wife were killed in Las Vegas. That's when things started to change, and not for the better," I said, amazed that I was bringing up these sad memories.

"Would you like to tell me about it?" Leslie asked.

"You know, I would. I'm finally ready to talk about that terrible time. It almost killed me, both physically and mentally."

"Let's go into the kitchen, Just throw your robe on over your pajamas and we'll have a big breakfast and a long talk."

I did what she said, then followed her into the kitchen and sat in a rocking chair that looked like the Amish had made it. I told Leslie the sad story, which had been one reason I had come to England. I wanted to go to a place where I could have peace, quiet and not be involved in anything that was related to violence of any sort.

"May, I think you're here for a reason, don't you? It's not the one you wanted, of course, but something out there in the netherworld wanted you around."

"Why me? I'm not part of this world – most of it I don't even understand," I said as I buttered another roll. I still sat in the rocker and Leslie had put a small table next to me and it was loaded with delicious food. Eggs, sausage, bacon, oatmeal, tomatoes, those yummy yeast rolls and cinnamon buns, still warm from the oven, with cream cheese frosting melting on top.

"I don't know the why of it, May, I just know it's happening the way it was meant to be."

"Sounds peculiar. And another thing – I'm eating like a horse. If this keeps up, I'll be too fat for my clothes."

"You need to gain about a stone to be truly healthy, so that's my goal before you leave us for America. When you fly away, you'll be back to your old self, only better," Leslie said as she poured more coffee in my cup and pushed the milk pitcher toward me.

"How much is a stone?" I asked as I licked cream cheese off my fingers.

"Fourteen pounds."

I looked up in horror and she laughed. It was a wonderful morning. Who cared if I gained a dress size or so? I reached for another helping of eggs, oatmeal, and bacon and sighed with total contentment.

Chapter Twenty-Five

The day went by in a blur of comfort, peace, quiet and food. When Leslie left for work, the refrigerator was filled with delicious meats, vegetables and desserts that I hadn't had since I was a child in Montana. In fact, the recipes seemed to be the same ones my mother had used.

As I ate my third piece of lemon pie made from sweetened condensed milk, egg yolks and lemon juice, I licked the three-inch meringue from my mouth and wondered how this English woman had the recipe. I'd have to ask her.

The night before I'd slept without any bad dreams. I didn't see Harvey's face, the way he'd looked in the morgue in Las Vegas. Even after the case was solved, the killer caught, it haunted me. And for years I'd had flashbacks to the time in Montana when both my parents had died because a drunk driver, going over one hundred miles an hour, ran head-long into their car.

I'd even told Leslie about Dan and our short-lived, disastrous marriage. Harvey, who was my partner on the Tacoma, Washington, police department, had tried to warn me about Dan. But I wouldn't listen...I loved him. When Dan left me for his secretary, who he'd gotten pregnant, Harvey and his first wife picked up the pieces. I did the same for him a few years later when she died of ovarian cancer.

I went outside, still in my pajamas, and sat on a little bench that was in the back garden. Mouser came up and jumped onto my lap, purring and so soft to the touch. I held him and thought some more about the past and then something inside of me seemed to lighten. It was like the heavy, sad feelings I had carried around for years evaporated. I'd never experienced anything like it and didn't understand how it happened. I just knew it had.

The sun was bright but the tall trees filtered it. They made a nice sound as a little wind blew through their leaves. The garden was interesting because, at least to my untrained eye, flowers from different seasons were growing together in a colorful jumble; red azaleas, yellow daffodils, white daisies, orange chrysanthemums, pink tulips, purple heather, black-eyed Susans. "There must be some sort of weather patterns around here that are different," I thought to myself.

I put Mouser down and we went into the house. Looking at the tub, I decided to take another soak, and so I did. Mouser lay on the floor, on his back, and his tummy soaked up a ray of sunshine that came through the window.

Like the night before, by the time Leslie came in, I had been asleep for hours and didn't hear her. My sleep was dreamless and when I woke, feeling even better than the day before, I looked forward to spending time with Leslie and asking her some of the questions I'd wondered about.

I smelled coffee so I padded into the kitchen. The pot was perking and there was a note from Leslie on the table.

"Had to go in early. Have a peaceful day. Want to have dinner at the pub tonight? If so, be there by seven. Love, Leslie"

The day went by like the day before. I dressed, fixed my hair and put on makeup for the first time in quite a while. I was at the pub a little before seven and it was packed with people.

I found my way to the back, selected the last empty table and sat down. I watched people for a while and then the door opened and Hamish Campbell walked in and looked around at the crowd. When he saw me, he lit up like a light bulb, waved, then walked in my direction.

"May, I'm so glad you called me back and asked me to join you tonight," he said as he pulled up a chair and sat down.

Before I could get a word out, Leslie appeared and set a cup of coffee in front of me. Hamish had a frosted glass with a foamy Guinness placed in front of him.

"I took the liberty of ordering for the two of you. It will be up in a little while," Leslie commented as she turned back to other customers who requested her attention.

"My goodness," I said, not knowing how to begin a conversation.

"I have news about the car wreck and fire, if you want to hear it," he said as he lifted his glass to take a long drink of the dark beer.

"Yes, please, let me know about it."

"It was an accident, pure and simple. Mrs. Foster had one of those electric-petrol hybrids and, as they do sometimes in a wreck, it blew up. We've had special training on how to handle those cars. They're great on petrol mileage but there are some dangerous bugs that need to be worked out. Anyway, it wasn't murder or anything like that."

"I met her mother and she'd told me it was an accident. Mrs. Owen said Amy's husband blamed himself because he'd talked her into that type of car. If I haven't missed it, I should go to the funeral." As I said this, I realized I hadn't thought about any of these things over the past two days.

"The funeral is tomorrow, in the village church. Her family is devastated, of course, and her mother is taking care of the little ones for the time being. Her husband is so broken up he can't function, even though we have explained to him he shouldn't feel responsible." Hamish looked down at his hands, which were on the table.

I noticed he had black hairs on his hands, not too much, just enough. I looked up and he was looking at me. "I knew you'd call," he said. "When I got the message telling me you couldn't meet me for dinner, I was disappointed, but not too much because I knew I'd hear from you." His smile was wide and his white, even teeth were punctuated on each side of his cheeks by small dimples. I wanted to kiss them. As I thought this, I blushed.

"You're blushing," he said. "Why?"

"Oh, dear," I said, wondering what was happening to me. Had I called this man? I didn't recall doing that. I'd thought it was behind me, that I was safe from these feelings.

"Not much of an answer," he said, and reached again for the Guinness.

"I've had a confusing couple of days; pleasant but unbelievable. You're Scottish but working in England?" I asked, hoping to get to easier topics of conversation.

"Yes and no."

This wasn't getting easier. "How so?" I asked.

"I beg you pardon?" he asked, looking as perplexed as I felt.

"I meant, what do you mean by 'yes and no?'"

"I am a Scottish firefighter who is currently working in England but only for a little while. Then I go home to Aberdeen."

"Which is north of Edinburgh," I said, hoping to score points for my knowledge of Scottish geography.

"Sort of. Really it's Northwest, but close enough. Have you been to Scotland?" He was looking around the room as he asked.

Thinking he was getting bored I replied, "No." I had neither the time nor interest in entertaining this man, even if I did want to kiss his dimples.

"May, we're off on a rabbit hunt and it's not rabbit season," he said, rubbing his hands along the side of the glass.

"I have no idea what you just said," I answered.

Leslie showed up at that moment, laden with plates piled high with pork loin, rice with gravy, green beans with sautéed mushrooms and more of those yeast rolls I craved.

"Are you two having fun?" she asked, hands on her hips.

"Yes," he replied.

"No," I said at the same time.

Leslie looked from one to the other, said, "How nice!" and left us to deal with dinner.

Both of us ate everything on our plates. Since we were eating so much, there really wasn't time to talk. So we didn't.

After he finished, Hamish looked at me, and said, "I like to see a woman who has a good appetite."

Before I could comment, the last person in the world I wanted to see bounded up to the table.

"Here you are, Eva May. I've been looking all over this burg for you. Mind if I sit down?" He sat, then stuck his hand out to Hamish and said, "I'm Dan Peterman, Eva May's husband. And you are?"

Chapter Twenty-Six

I left soon after Hamish and drove the short distance back to Leslie's house. Dan was still at the bar, regaling people with lies. He and Hamish hit it off and I got very bored listening to them bond. I promised both Hamish and Dan I'd call them tomorrow. On my way to Leslie's, I'd decided to forget those promises.

I changed out of my skirt and blouse and put on my pajamas and robe. It dawned on me as I did this that I hadn't heard from DC Johnston for the last few days.

I went over to my purse, dug around inside, and pulled out my cell phone. For some reason I couldn't get a signal. I went over to the telephone that sat on a desk in the living room, picked up the receiver and it was dead, too.

"Strange," I said out loud

Another thing was I knew I hadn't called Hamish and asked him to have dinner with me. That had to be a set up, and it must have been Leslie who called him.

Tomorrow I would go to Amy Foster's funeral. It was horrible the way she had died but at least she hadn't been murdered.

I had every intention of waiting for Leslie but as soon as I lay down on the bed, just for a moment I told myself, I was out for the night.

* * *

When I woke the following morning, Leslie was gone, and there was no note. I made coffee, ate fruit and cheese, and then got ready to go into the village. I didn't know the time of the funeral but I needed to do a few errands anyway. The main thing was to get my cell phone working again. It had been nice being off line for a while, but I was ready to get back into the world. I loved Leslie's house, but it truly was outside the mainstream of everything. Now that I looked around, there wasn't a TV or radio or computer in sight. It had taken me three days to notice that. I must have needed rest more than I'd thought.

I used Leslie's washer and dryer to do a small load of clothes. In the meantime, I cleaned up and dressed for the funeral. Also, I made the decision to leave and find accommodations elsewhere. It had been wonderful, but I felt the need to move on. I cleaned up the house as best as I could, trying to leave it just as I found it.

I wrote Leslie a long, enthusiastic note thanking her for the gracious hospitality and kindness. I would stop at the florist and have a large bouquet of flowers sent to her. Thinking about that, I didn't have an address so I looked around for a bill or some other item that might have an address on it, but I didn't find anything. None of the glossy magazines had an address label, so she must have bought those in a shop in the village. I went outside and looked around, but there were no numbers on the house and there was no place that I saw to deliver mail. But then, she probably picked it up in the village at the post office. I guess I could send it to the pub, but would prefer that the flowers came to the house.

Before I left, I had hoped to see Mouser but he hadn't been around all day. It was sad to leave, but I knew it was time. Leslie had done enough to help me and I needed to go back out into the world.

Her home was truly a place like I'd never been before. If the house had a name, it should be called "Sanctuary."

I put my bags in the car, went back inside long enough to take another look around the glorious rooms, left the key on top of the note I'd written her, then closed the door. I jiggled the door just to make sure it was secure then I got in my car and drove into the village, which took about five minutes.

There was a parking spot near the grocery and I pulled in with no trouble. I took my cell phone from my purse and had a strong signal. Before I went into the grocery, I called DC Johnston and asked that he call me back. I also called Leslie at the pub and told her I'd locked up and left her home, thanking her profusely. She was gracious and told me to return any time I needed peace and quiet.

After I got inside the store, I realized I'd forgotten to get her address. I picked up a few items and went to the checkout.

The same lady whose sister owned the B&B was working at the checkout. "I was hoping I'd see you here today," I told her, placing shampoo and hand lotion on the counter.

"Oh, it's you. Haven't seen you in a little while. Thought you'd gone home to America," she said as she rang up my bill.

"Do you know if your sister might have a room for me at her B&B? I know she was filled up a couple of days ago."

She looked surprised. "Not that I heard her say. In fact, she put an advert in the local paper because she was short of guests. No one else is in line, let me give her a quick jingle." She picked up the telephone that was next to the register and dialed the number.

"Helen, hello? It's me. Listen, Dear, I have a nice American lady who needs a room. Don't you have availability? That's what I thought. I'll send her over, luv. Ta ta."

She put the telephone down and then gave me directions to the B&B.

I thanked her, picked up my small parcel and started to leave when I heard a familiar voice call, "May! Can we talk?"

Steven Roberts loped toward me and I dreaded a conversation with him. Something about this hulk of a man put me off. I couldn't for the life of me understand why Sarah Demming had been so charmed by him. Perhaps he'd just aged badly.

By the time he'd got to me he was out of breath and had to take a moment to wheeze.

I did my best not to look bored. "Hello again, Mr. Roberts," I said, taking a step back. This man always stood too close, just like he had in the shoe shop.

"It's delightful to see you again, May. Please call me Steven."

"How can I help you, Mr. Roberts?" I asked, hoping he got the point.

"Would you like to accompany me to the movies? I believe I mentioned that to you once before. It's a very good murder mystery," he said, his nose glowing red and sweaty.

"Mr. Roberts, I don't care for mysteries. But thank you anyway. Good day." I continued to step backward, turned and tried not to run out of the shop.

Before I could get around to the driver door of the car and get in he was almost on top of me.

"No need to be rude, Miss. I'm just trying to be friendly." His big smile looked wolfish.

"Thank you again, Mr. Roberts." I got in the car and locked the door. I hoped he'd heard the locks click.

I pulled out of the parking spot and drove down the street. Rounding a curve, out of sight of the grocery, I took the first open spot I found and parked the car.

Before I could get out and go into the florist shop, my cell phone rang. Pulling it out of my bag, I answered on the third ring. "Hello?"

"DC Johnston here. Where have you been, May? I've been trying to locate you for three days."

"I've been with Leslie at her house. I left a message for you," I said.

"Well, I never received it. Where are you now? We need to talk."

"I'm sitting in front of the florist shop in the village. What time is Amy's funeral?" I asked.

"It's at eleven this morning. Are you going?" he said.

"Yes, I'll see you there. We could talk afterwards, if you'd like."

"Good. See you then."

I was certain I'd left him a message telling him I was staying with Leslie. But then, I'd been out of it for the past few days so I wasn't sure what I had or hadn't done. I got out of the car and entered the florist shop, which was crowded. Eventually a harried clerk waited on me. I ordered a huge bouquet of summer flowers and, because no one could track down Leslie's home address, had them sent to the pub.

I had about an hour before the funeral so I called the B&B and reserved a room. She gave me directions and I told her I'd stop by in the early afternoon to check in. Now that that was settled, I decided just to walk about and be a tourist in the village.

It was very pleasant, mild weather and the High Street wasn't too busy. I went into the post office and asked if they could give me Leslie's home address. They tracked it down for me and I considered returning to the florist and changing the delivery address but decided to leave it as it was. She spent more time at the pub than she did at home, anyway.

There was a small park across from the church and I walked around, looking at the pretty flowers, and after that sat on a bench. I had a clear view of the front of the church and I saw that people were beginning to arrive for Amy Foster's funeral. It hadn't been that long since I first met her in line at the grocery. That had been my first day in town. It was hard to believe she was dead. It was going to be a full church, based on the number of people who were arriving.

Some of them I recognized. I started to walk across the street when I saw DC Johnston's car arrive. I waited for him as he parked and got out of his car. We said hello and went into the church together. As I suspected, we sat on the back pew. The church was filled and Amy's casket was in place at the base of the raised pulpit.

When the family came in, we rose as they walked to their seats at the front. The ceremony was somber and quiet. This wasn't a "life celebration" as in recent funerals I'd attended in the U.S. In some ways, I preferred this staid, somber ceremony. It was such a tragic loss of a young life that standing up and making upbeat comments about the positive aspects of this young woman would have seemed out of place. People loved Amy–that was clear by the filled church pews.

DC Johnston and I were among the last to file out after the service ended. Amy was to be buried in the graveyard behind the church, the same one where Sarah Demming had been laid to rest so many years ago.

Chapter Twenty-Seven

After the service, we walked back to the park and took a seat on the same bench I'd sat on before the service.

"How have you been?" he asked, as he continued to watch the crowd from across the street. Police officers were directing traffic as people got into their cars and left the area. The internment was private, with only Amy's immediate family in attendance. There was to be a gathering at her mother's home later in the afternoon. I wasn't sure if I would go to that or not. I hadn't decided.

"I've been out of the loop for the last few days and I feel better for it; I hibernated at Leslie's house. Do you think I should go to the gathering?"

"I'm going. But it's part of the job. You can go with me, if you like," he said, still observing the crowd that was starting to thin.

"I'm checking into the B&B where Dan is staying, although I wish he'd get on the first jet back to Seattle."

"You push people away, don't you May? Do you know you do it or is it unconscious behavior on your part?" he looked directly at me when he asked this.

"Let me think about this. I have an answer but I'm wondering why it's any of your business?" I responded.

He raised an eyebrow. "Ouch!"

"Now, what did you want to talk to me about, other than a psychological profile of my bad behavior?"

"Amy's death was an accident. Her hybrid car blew up when it crashed," he said.

"I know."

He looked at me again. "How?"

"Mrs. Owen, Amy's mother, told me and then Hamish Campbell mentioned it when we had dinner last night."

"Ah, Mr. Campbell our Scottish firefighter. And how was dinner?"

"The food was great but we didn't get along. Then Dan showed up and those two became BFF's in a second," I said, looking down at my hands.

"Let me make a wild guess. You pushed both of them away."

"Sort of. I'll admit to a little bit of that. I just don't want to get involved in any way with anyone. Even you." I said and looked him right in the eyes.

"You're lying, May. You and I both know that when someone looks you right in the eye they're fibbing."

"That's not always the truth and it's not in this case. You're just mad because I wouldn't go stay at your house."

"That was a perfectly innocent invitation. I live with my mother."

I couldn't help it. I laughed. "You live with your mother?"

"Yes, and it works for both of us. She was looking forward to meeting you, by the way."

He was perfectly at ease talking about this. I liked it. I might have to change my opinion of DC Johnston.

"I'd love to meet her."

"Go check into your B&B, meet me at the gathering and afterwards I'll take you home to meet her. You can have dinner with us and I promise it won't be like last night."

"How's that?" I asked, thinking I knew what he'd say.

"Because the food will be terrible. Neither my mother nor I can cook anything that will be remotely edible."

I left him and drove to the B&B. It was a pretty place located in a broad area of open land, what would be called a moor in England. In Montana, where I had lived for my first eighteen years, it would be called a cow pasture.

The house was built of the yellowish stone that was common to the area. The stones glowed in the early afternoon sun as if they were lit from within. A rock wall enclosed the area around the house and several outbuildings. The entire place looked like it belonged to a different era. Unlike Leslie's cottage, there were no tall trees around this house.

When I got out of the Land Rover, I stood for a few moments and looked in all directions, because the property was built on a slight hill. In some ways, it was more beautiful than the cottage I had stayed in for the past few nights.

I heard a door open and turned to the sound of a woman's voice, "Come, Miss Scott. Let's get you settled in."

A matronly woman who looked remarkably like the lady from the grocery walked toward me. "I'm Helen Waddle. You've already met my twin sister, Ellen. Welcome to our home," she beamed, pulling me into a bear hug.

Whoever said the English were standoffish must have been in a different part of the country.

She helped bring my bags in, although I tried to discourage her. I followed in the wake of her ample rump as she went up the steep stairs faster than I ever could.

The room was well used but clean and perfectly acceptable. I went over to the window and looked out over the moor and thought of Charlotte Bronte's memorable characters Jane Eyre and Mr. Rochester.

"I'm afraid you'll have to share a loo but we only have the one guest and he's gone most of the time."

"Is his name Dan?" I asked, hoping that he had left.

"Why, yes. Do you two know each other?" Helen Waddle asked, her nose twitching.

"Yes, we do know each other." I smiled and wished I'd taken DC Johnston up on his offer.

"He's such a delightful man. Don't you agree?" she beamed.

"Could you show me where the loo is located?" I asked, hoping to divert her attention.

"Of course, it's right out in the hall to your left. It's between your two rooms," she added, raising her eyebrows.

I decided right then I'd stay one night and then move on. In fact, Maple Cottage was starting to appeal to me, even with the specter of the snake still in my head. Rodney was probably out of the hospital by now so I decided to go visit him at the manor house and ask if I could have the key back. I had, after all, paid him for two months at the cottage. Before I did that, though, I'd call just to make sure Rodney was there. If not, I'd have to make the trip into Swindon and the hospital.

Miss Waddle vacated the room and I decided not to unpack a thing since my tenure here would be so short. If I played my cards right, I could avoid Dan altogether, along with the landlady. I had to wonder what it was like when Ellen came home from her job at the grocery and joined her sister Helen to run the B&B. There had been a little bit of deceptive advertising on the part of Ellen, who never made it clear she was part of the operation, too. Oh, well, I'd be gone in less than twenty-four hours.

I ran a comb through my hair, applied lip gloss and locked the bedroom door behind me. I also had a key to the front door, but I left that unlocked. Moving fast, I got into the car and drove away before Helen tracked me down and started asking more Dan questions.

I followed the directions DC Johnston had given me and found myself at Amy's childhood home in about fifteen minutes. It was in the direction of Glastonbury, territory that I'd not explored yet. When I had been in high school the novels of Marian Zimmer Bradley about this region had been my favorite reading material. Everywhere I went in the area brought me face to face with those wonderful books and seeing the surroundings made the characters come to life.

DC Johnston was there, waiting for me outside of his car. "Did you get settled in?" he asked.

"Yes, and I'll be there one night. I discovered the secret of Ellen and Helen Waddle."

"I thought it best for you to come to your own conclusions about that," he said, grinning.

We walked up stone steps to a small house surrounded by beech trees. They were very tall and graceful. I stood for a moment before we went in and listened to the sound they made as the wind blew through their branches. It looked like a wonderful place to grow up. The sad part was Amy was so young when she died. "If she only hadn't come to meet me," I said.

"Don't blame yourself for her death, May. It was a terrible auto accident, nothing to do with any of these other incidents," DC Johnston said as he took my arm and led me into the home.

I offered my condolences to Mrs. Owen and the rest of her family, took a cup of coffee and stood by the front window. In a few minutes, she joined me.

"I never found the letters, Miss Scott. But I've looked everywhere. If you do find out anything else about Amy's death, will you please tell me?" she asked.

"I most certainly will. You must understand, though, that I'm just a tourist. Detective Constable Johnston is in charge of the investigation. He's worked very long and hard on this case. I believe you've talked to him on several occasions?"

"He's been wonderful to our family," she said. A new crop of visitors arrived and she thanked me for coming and went back to her family.

I hadn't seen Amy's husband before and I watched him. He seemed to be in a dazed state and I wondered if he had been put on tranquillizers to get him through the day. He was a small man in stature, thin, and looked old for his age, which I thought was somewhere in the forties.

DC Johnston spoke with several people, had something to eat, then came and joined me. "Are you ready to leave, May?" he asked, looking back over the people who had crowded into the small home.

"Yes, I'm going to contact Rodney and ask if I can move back into the cottage."

"Let's go outside to talk about that," he said and we moved toward the door.

"Should we say good-bye to the family?" I asked. But it was evident they were surrounded by people and wouldn't notice we had left.

"Please come sit with me in my car for a few moments, May," he said as we walked toward our cars.

"We do need to chat. There are so many loose ends and questions I have. I wonder if you have any answers yet?" I asked, as I opened the left side front door of his unmarked police car.

"First, Lord Willsdon is back at home, even though we requested that he not move back in. And I would ask that you not move back into the cottage. It's just not safe for you. We have an on going investigation into the death of Mrs. Long, his housekeeper, and then there are the bones from the body that was discovered along that hidden road beside the manor house. I believe you were there that night when the young constable found it."

"Yes, I was. I'd never even noticed that road and it was next to the cottage and the garden shed. Bushes and trees hid it. Now that I know it's there, I can recognize it as a road. Have you found any evidence that will point toward the killer? And have the bones been identified?"

DC Johnson sighed, "We've sent the bones and the surrounding soil to Scotland Yard. They're so behind, though, it will take time before we hear anything. We have found some facts about Mrs. Long, however. I, for one, wasn't aware she'd worked for Lord and Lady Willsdon, the current Lord Willsdon's parents. Also, she had been dead several hours by the time you and Dan found her."

"That surprises me. Somehow I had the impression Mrs. Long hadn't been dead that long. Of course, I checked only enough to make sure she wasn't still breathing. And I thought you'd grown up in the village so you'd have known that she'd worked at the manor house for years," I said.

"When my dad passed, almost two years ago, I moved with my mother to this area. She has a sister not far away and that's what she wanted. I'm a London boy, through and through. I got a transfer from the London Metro Police to here and started back to work immediately after we got settled."

"So I guess all this fresh air and open country isn't your cuppa," I responded.

His laugh sounded first-rate and I knew how seldom he felt like laughing, with the career path he had decided to follow. "If I had my way I'd be meandering my way through the grimy streets of London right this minute."

"Why don't you tell your mother that and go back to London?" I asked. "I left Montana at eighteen and never went back, except for visits. You don't have to live with your mother, you know."

"Well, there's that promise I made to my dad on his deathbed–to watch out for her, take care of her. I won't go back on my word. Anyway, I'm learning to like the area, sort of."

"Is there any evidence of how Mrs. Long died? It looked like a gunshot wound to me. Was it?" I asked, nosy as always.

"Yes, but we can't find a weapon. We've searched again and again with no luck. That's part of the reason we don't want Lord Willsdon in there"

"Then don't let him in. You have the power, DC Johnston–use it. It's a crime scene and it belongs to you and your teams."

He shook his head and looked sad, "Ah, spoken like a true American. You don't understand the gentry. I'd say it's like a Laird in Scotland but that wouldn't make sense to you either, would it?"

"Not really. I suppose Rodney is the 'pooh-bah Lord-High-Everything- Else' like in Gilbert and Sullivan's 'The Mikado,'" I said.

"Yes, but even more than that. He carries the weight of the village on his shoulders and so far, as you have noticed, this is a prosperous place. In fact, it astounds me how well the village does. Perhaps if it was the opposite he wouldn't have such power, but he does and there isn't a way around it that I can find," DC Johnston said.

"I can't believe I'm listening to an officer of the law tell me that one handicapped veteran rules everything," I said.

"It's a closed, ancient society in a lot of ways. And since I'm a newcomer, I'm a definite outsider, just like you, May. Your entrée has been because you're American and an attractive female. Doors open easier for you because of it," he commented as he shifted in the comfortable leather seat.

"Amy made somewhat the same comment to me, about the fact I was an outsider. She also said she wanted to protect her baby. Was she pregnant" I asked.

"I don't know. I'll have that checked. She might have been referring to her young children–they're not much older than babies."

"Yes, but I thought when she said it that she meant she was pregnant – that's how I took the comment. Maybe that means something, although at this point I have no clue what it could be."

"By the way, the snake didn't belong to Swindon Zoo, as we thought," he said, "it actually came from Cranfield University's science lab."

"That's intriguing," I said. "I visited Cranfield University with Rodney soon after I arrived. He works there teaching classes to military students from around the world."

"Yes, I know. That's also where your Scottish bagpiper has been staying. He's in residence there for classes in fire science. That's why Hamish Campbell is here this summer. He serves as a fireman for Swindon on a volunteer basis."

"How did you know he played the bagpipes?" I asked.

"Oh, I know everything about everybody, you know that."

"You didn't know about Mrs. Long," I couldn't resist saying.

"That's right. But I do now," he responded, as he reached for his ringing mobile phone.

I waved goodbye and got out of his car. By the time I got to the Land Rover and had buckled the seatbelt, I remembered I wanted to ask if anything had been determined about the explosion that had killed Michael Reed, Rodney's solicitor.

That's where all of this had started.

.

Chapter Twenty-Eight

Since the afternoon was so nice and I didn't want to go back to the B&B until it was late, I turned the car toward Glastonbury. When I got into the city center, I stopped at a tourist information office and got a map of the local sights.

I spent a couple of hours visiting Glastonbury Abbey, which was erected on the site of the first Christian church in Britain, built by Joseph of Arimathea. It is also the supposed burial site for King Arthur.

The grounds of the Abbey were green and peaceful parkland, with many unusual species of trees, including a small cider apple orchard. I was surprised to learn that the word Avalon means apple.

Chalice Well was my next stop and it lies in a stunning garden, interspersed with several water pools. My favorite section of the grounds was King Arthur's Chalice. The water made a soothing, rippling sound as it cascaded over the reddish stones and the garden lent itself to quiet contemplation.

I had planned on visiting other legendary sites in Glastonbury, but the healing, meditative waters of the Chalice Well made me change my mind. I stayed until early evening, when the garden closed.

I found a small restaurant and went in for a simple meal. As I ate, I promised myself I'd return and continue my tour of the Isle of Avalon, also known as Glastonbury.

It was late by the time I got back to the B&B. I saw another car in the drive but it didn't look like Dan's rental. Making as little noise as possible, I crept up the stairs to my room.

I took off my clothes, put on my bathrobe and gathered my bath items. Opening the door just a crack, I peered out into the hall with one eye. It was quiet so I quickly made my way into the bathroom and firmly locked the door.

Unlike Leslie's, where I spent lots of time in the tub, I took a shower, washed my hair and was out of there in fifteen minutes. It reminded me of getting ready for work. I made a quick swipe to clean the tub and sink then was out the door and back in my room.

I pulled out my hair dryer and quickly blew my hair dry. I felt much better and pulled on my comfy flannel pants and shirt that says "Hairy Potter" on the front. Janet, my best friend from Las Vegas, gave it to me for my last birthday. She knew I was trying to improve the little garden around my house and was having fun doing it. It's amazing what will grow in the desert when you add water to the mix.

I crawled into bed, pulled the covers up and promptly went to sleep.

When I woke up the next morning sunshine streamed into the room. I stayed in bed, not quite awake, and tried to figure out if the conversation I had with Sarah Demming was real or a dream. I smelled coffee so I must be awake. I sat up and looked around the room. It was all just as I'd left it the night before.

Somehow, I had met with her at Stonehenge. I found myself sitting on a flat outcropping of aged rock. The sky was just starting to change into early morning and there were swirls of pink with a backdrop of pale yellow. It wasn't cold and when I glanced down at my clothes, I was wearing pajamas. Looking around, Salisbury Plain was quiet, and there was no traffic on the roadway. The single chain that kept the tourists at a polite distance didn't circle Stonehenge.

In the distance, I saw a woman walking toward me. As she approached, I realized it was Sarah Demming. When she got to the place where I sat, I saw that she was a pretty, blonde teenager with startling blue eyes and skin like peaches and cream. Her clothes, from the sixties, reminded me of photos I'd seen of my mother from that period, before I was born.

Sarah was talking to me and it was like I heard her through a static-filled radio. I could make out every third word or so. I kept saying, "I can't understand you." About that time Leslie walked up, from which direction I couldn't tell, and said, "Let me help." She sat down next to me on the hard gray rock and then I could understand Sarah's voice.

"I love him but you have to stop him. He doesn't know what he's doing. It's not his fault. Please make him stop before he kills again. I want him with me, that's all I've ever wanted. He's ill, so mentally sick, and he needs me. Please send him home to me," Sarah pleaded, tears streaming down her young face.

Then, before my eyes, she faded slowly away. Leslie took my hand and said, "May, can you help Sarah?"

"I'll try," I said, having no idea what I was supposed to do.

I got out of bed and the dream was fading away, as Sarah had done. I got a pen and a piece of paper and wrote down everything I could recall before it all disappeared like fog on the moor.

Dressing quickly, I put the few items I'd taken out back into my suitcase, made the room presentable, then took my bag down the stairs and out to my car. I went back into the house, entered the dining room and helped myself to the breakfast that was on the sideboard.

I wasn't hungry but, remembering that Leslie told me I needed to eat a healthier diet, I ate a respectable breakfast. The coffee was weak but drinkable and I was having my second cup when Dan walked in.

"So we meet again," he said. "I heard you come in last night but, as you can see, I was a total gentleman and let you have your privacy."

"Thank you for that. I didn't see your car."

"It's in the building in the back. Ellen and Helen told me all about you, by the way." He headed for the food. "They really like me, May."

"I can see the attraction," I said. "When are you leaving England?"

"The Waddle girls want me to stay here and be a handyman. I just might do it for a month or two. What do you think?" he asked as he piled his plate high with eggs, sausages, bacon and muffins.

"You don't have a handy bone in your body, Dan. I think it's perfect for you. Stay here a long time."

"Really? I thought you'd be jealous. These are good-looking, wealthy women here."

"Check out the work visa rules and stay, Dan. I wish you all the best. Now, I have to go," I said, pushing out of the chair. "Could you tell the Waddles' it was my pleasure to spend the night but I've made other accommodations? Here's the key, Handyman. See you around." I laid the key on the table and headed for the door.

"Bye," Dan called as he tucked into his food.

Fully expecting him to run after me, I was surprised. He didn't.

"Now why does that bother me?" I asked myself as I pulled out of the driveway and headed for the motorway.

I planned on stopping at the manor house to visit Rodney and ask for the cottage key, but before I did that I wanted to talk to Joan Pritchard, Librarian. She was related to Sarah. Maybe if I looked over the newspaper articles concerning Sarah's death, and the village legend that was built around it, possibly I could make sense of the dream.

It was early enough that I found a place to park in front of the library. I got out of the car and walked toward the door. When I pushed it open, Joan, who was behind the counter, called a cheery "Hello."

"Good morning," I said as I walked up to her. "I know I've asked you this before, but could I see the news articles and the tourist brochure you have about Sarah Demming?"

Joan looked at me over her spectacles and asked, "Is she still haunting you at Maple Cottage?"

"Sort of. I'm just trying to figure it out. Somehow, the pieces I have don't complete the puzzle," I said as I put my purse on top of the counter.

"Let me go find that for you. I might still have it out from the last time you visited," she said, and headed for the archive section.

She was back in a few minutes with the requested information. "Do you want to take this folder over to a table and make yourself comfortable? If you need anything else, let me know." The telephone was ringing in the office so she went to answer it.

I took the folder and sat at a table near a window that looked out to the High Street. It was getting busier, but nothing like Swindon or Glastonbury.

Before I started reading through the clippings and booklet, I let my mind wander to what I knew about Sarah Demming. She was a teenager who got pregnant by her boyfriend, the current owner of the grocery. He denied he was the father but that was the gossip that swirled around the village. Sarah, trying to abort the baby, accidentally killed herself. She haunted Maple Cottage, part of the manor house property, so often that she became a local legend. Ghost hunters came to the village on a regular basis to search for her ghost, who supposedly only appeared to women. Her body was buried in the church cemetery, next to her father.

That's when I remembered. Sarah's mother was still alive. Maybe she could help me understand the dream.

I took the folder back to the counter and waited for Joan to come back from the office. When she did, I asked if she knew where Mrs. Rachel Demming currently resided. "I'd heard she was in a care facility. Is that true?"

"No, she's in a convent in Glastonbury. We go see her occasionally. Let me get the address and telephone number for you. I'm sure she'd be delighted to have a visitor."

This wasn't what I expected. I thought I'd be told to stay away. "How does she react to the fact her daughter is, supposedly, a ghost?" I asked the librarian.

"You know, we never talk about it. It's as though that part of her life never happened. We discuss current goings on with our family, but never those days. I don't think she knows about Sarah being a ghost. You aren't going to tell her, are you? If that's the case, I don't think it's a good idea for you to see her. Please, let her live in the world she knows. She's a happy person." Joan's hands were clinched on the edge of the counter and her eyes pleaded with me not to upset the delicate balance.

"I'll do my best not to cause her pain in any way," I lied. I knew I had to ask the questions Joan didn't want me to. I knew no other way, though, to get to the truth. This whole story of Sarah didn't add up.

Anyway, I'd made a promise to Leslie and Sarah to solve this mystery. I couldn't let them down, even if it was only a dream.

Joan provided the information on how to contact Rachel Demming. I thanked her and left before she could come up with more reasons why I shouldn't pursue the visit.

When I got back in my car, I called the manor house and left a message for Rodney, asking that I be allowed to take the cottage back for the time I'd contracted. I had hoped to talk to him but the phone rang repeatedly until the recorder device came on. I told him I was going into Glastonbury to talk with Mrs. Demming about Sarah and that I would be late arriving. The key could be placed in the small birdhouse that was in the branches of the rose arbor next to the front door, I told him.

It was an easy drive to the convent, as I had already made my way through Glastonbury yesterday. In fact, I drove by the Chalice Well and the convent was only a little farther down the two-lane road. I wondered if Mrs. Demming spent time in the gardens.

I pulled into the car park, shut the engine off and pulled out my cell phone. I dialed the number Joan had given me and it was answered within two rings. I asked if I could visit with Mrs. Demming and was told I could. I was to check in at the office and they would bring her to me.

I locked the car and found the office. When I opened the door, a bell tinkled. A sister of the convent came out and spoke with me. She had been the one I talked to. While I signed in, she went through a side door, telling me she would return momentarily. As I watched her walk away, she reminded me of the sisters who used to serve in the church I had attended as a child in Montana. After my parent's were killed, I didn't go back and sometimes I missed it. My grandfather never made me go with him, although he attended Mass every Sunday.

The office was small but modern. There was a computer sitting on the desk next to the counter, which was newer than anything I've ever used. It looked out of place in the old building. They must have done a great deal of renovation to get all of this new technology wired into the building. I peeped into the office and was surprised to see a wall-mounted flat screen TV. "My goodness," I said out loud. This was the most up to date, modern facility I'd seen in England.

Hearing quiet footsteps, I looked toward the sound and two sisters walked into the room. "I'm Sister Martha. How can I serve you?" she asked.

"I'll leave you two alone now. Sister Martha, perhaps your guest would like a cup of tea?"

Sister Martha turned to her and said, "Thank you, Sister Ruth, that's an excellent idea."

"Come this way, please," Sarah's mother said to me.

I was beginning to feel like I'd fallen though Alice's rabbit hole, where nothing was as it seemed.

I followed her small figure through brick arched doors into a garden. "Since the weather is so pleasant would you care to sit out here?" she asked politely.

"Yes, that would be fine. My name is May Scott, by the way."

She turned to me then and said, "I know who you are. Joan Pritchard called a little while ago and told me you'd be coming." Her voice was gentle and her smile was kind. "Please, sit here and I'll bring tea for us," she indicated a small round stone table with benches on each side.

I sat and wondered how I could be so crass as to ask this devout woman about her dead daughter, who had either performed a botched abortion on herself or was murdered and now wandered around haunting people.

Sister Martha returned with a tea tray and cookies. She sat them on the table and took a seat across from me. "Please, Miss Scott, have a biscuit. Do you take anything in your tea?" she asked as she poured the fragrant brew into a dainty yellow china cup that sat on a matching saucer.

"Nothing, thanks," I said as I accepted the cup and saucer. I looked longingly at the cookies but knew I was just putting off what I didn't want to do.

So I began. "Did Mrs. Pritchard tell you why I wanted to see you, Sister Martha?"

"No," she answered and looked at me with those startling blue eyes just like Sarah's that I remembered from my dream.

She was smaller than her daughter, who had been tall, but I could see where the beautiful complexion and blonde hair came from. There were wisps of light hair around the modified habit that she wore. Of course, her hair was probably gray by now, I thought as I observed her and drank my tea.

"This tea smells delicious," I commented, delaying the conversation.

"Yes, it's hibiscus." She looked at me and said, "Ask your questions, Miss Scott. I've known this day was coming and I've been ready to answer for years."

"Can you tell me what happened to Sarah?" I said.

The place where we sat was, as so many other gardens were in England, green and beautiful. The trees were ancient and their branches reached upward. Between the canopies of green, the blue sky peeked though. There weren't as many flowers here as in other gardens I'd visited, but there were pieces of sculpture at various points around the enclosed area. A high stone wall circled the convent and there were no road noises, as we were off the main highway.

She told me the heartbreaking story from so many years before. In some ways, it was more horrifying than I'd imagined. When she finished, she reached across the table and covered my hands with hers. "Tell my daughter's story, Miss Scott. It's time all of this sadness came to an end."

Chapter Twenty-Nine

After I left the convent I returned to the small café I'd stopped at the evening before. It was quiet and I ordered a salad and coffee.

I wanted time to sit and think about what I'd heard. Part of it was inconceivable, but I believed every word Sister Martha said. I had asked her why she hadn't gone to the police and she said she thought they would come to her, and it never happened. So she had melted away into the convent and had created a productive, peaceful life.

During a visit to Sedona, Arizona, I had become familiar with vortexes – ley lines configured along the earth's surface that brought concentrated power to an area. I knew that Stonehenge, Glastonbury and Avebury formed a potent vortex in the English West Country. I think I had just witnessed another type of persuasive vortex, created by Leslie, Sarah, and Sister Martha.

The drive back to the village took longer than the night before because of tourist traffic, but I welcomed it. I needed time to figure out what to do with the information I had.

By the time I pulled into the Maple Cottage driveway, I had a plan in place. Pulling out my phone from my purse, I put in a call to DC Johnston. It went to his voice mail, as I figured it would.

I got out of the car, locked it, and headed toward the rose trellis to find the key in the birdhouse. It wasn't there so I searched a couple more times with no luck. I tried the door anyway, but it was locked. Walking around to the back, I had no success with the backdoor, either. I tried not to, but I had to look in the direction of the garden shed. I hoped the rattlesnake was back in his lab at the university and lived a long, happy reptile life away from me.

I called DC Johnston again and left another message. I knew he was going to be very glad when I departed the country.

Sighing, I headed toward the manor house. When I got through the avenue of trees and could see the house, it was dark. Perhaps Rodney hadn't left the hospital after all, I thought. I never had liked the looks of this place from the first time I saw it. The grounds were spectacular but the design of the house left me cold.

I walked around to the rear, thinking the back door would be open, but it wasn't. There was no welcoming greeting from Jazz, either. Going back to the front of the house, I climbed the steep steps that lead to the huge double doors and rang the bell. I could hear it echoing throughout the house. I waited a few minutes, tried the bell again, but still no response.

The windows were dark but it felt like eyes were watching me on all sides. It was a very eerie sensation and I didn't like it. There was only one other way I knew to gain entry and that was through the side door that Dan and I had discovered a few days ago. At that moment, I wished he were with me, if for nothing more than comic relief.

The steps were steep at the side of the house, with no railing to hold onto. Whoever had designed them didn't do it with safety or comfort in mind. When I got to the door and turned the handle, it opened. I stood there for a moment wondering if I should go in. Reluctantly, I did, going against all of my instincts. I should wait for DC Johnston.

It was dark in the hallway and when I pushed in the circle light switch, nothing happened. I felt my way along the wall and when I came to the hidden panel door, which was the pattern for the airline cart, I reached down to the bottom, and as Dan had showed me, slid the bolt back. Maybe he was handier than I thought. I quietly slid the panel open just a couple of inches and looked out into the gloomy vastness of the entry hall. A few more inches gave me a better view but all was quiet. "Jazz must be going home at night with a staff member," I thought. "Otherwise, he'd be here jumping up and greeting me." Opening the door all the way, I took a tentative step out onto the marble floor. I stood still and listened but there were no sounds.

I walked as quietly as possible to the door that led to where Rodney had gathered with his friends. I recall that Mrs. Long had taken me along the passageway to a set of doors on the left of the entry hall. The doors were shut and before I turned the handle I took a deep breath "Please protect me," I threw out to the cosmos. The handle moved, and I pushed the door open.

"Come in," a voice said. "I've been waiting for you."

I couldn't see anybody because the room was dark, no lights were on and the dark damask curtains were pulled shut. I turned in the direction of the voice. "I spoke with your grandmother today. She sends her love."

"I've never met her. Does she look like my mother?"

"Yes, except she's smaller. I think you look like her a bit."

"What did she say about me?"

"That you'd had a hard time of it and needed help. She'd like to be of assistance, if you'll let her."

"Did she send you here, May?"

"Three people sent me – your mother, grandmother, and Leslie."

"You spoke to my mother?"

"Yes, in a dream. That's how I talked to Leslie, too," I told him.

"Would you like to sit down?"

"Yes, Rodney, I'd like that very much. Could you turn on a light so I can find a chair?"

"Oh, excuse my bad manners." He clicked on a lamp and he sat in his wheelchair with a blanket over his lap.

"Are you cold?" I asked as I moved slowly to a chair. I didn't want to alarm or startle him in any way. I prayed silently that DC Johnston was on his way.

"When did you figure it out?" he asked.

"I'm not sure I have. That's why I thought perhaps you could explain it to me," I said, and folded my hands on my lap so he could see them. Somehow I had to take a look around the room and locate the airline cart.

Rodney said, "I found out about my mother, Sarah Demming, early on. I didn't look like the Lord and Lady and somehow I just didn't belong here, ever. They were kind, gave me everything but still there was emptiness. Do you know what I mean?"

"I think so," I said, shifting in the chair so perhaps I could get a glimpse of the room. "Did other people know?"

"Yes, many people in the village. This is a very insular place, more than you know."

"Why did you have to kill Michael Reed?" I asked.

"He knew too much. In the old days there was more of a group effort, now it's like I'm expected to go it alone."

"How?"

"I have to make sure the village is solvent, this pile is in the chips and I'm always the cheerful Lord of the Manor."

"That's what I mean, Rodney, how did you accomplish all that?"

"I have contacts throughout the world because of my job at the university. I've been their medical guinea pig, too. Did you know that?" he asked, grinning.

"No, I don't think I know very much about you at all, do I?"

He shook his head to indicate no and wheeled his chair closer to me. "It's possible to make lots of money by selling stolen and sometimes faked paintings. I hired a very talented painter, with no scruples but a raging alcohol addiction. When he was sober he did spectacular work for me. Then I have a cat burglar friend who, on occasion, steals the real thing. He also transported the items around Great Britain for me. You might have met him? Bruce Foster, Amy's husband. She never knew anything about it, though. I need cash and this way I can make lots of money. Have you seen the 'art gallery,' as I call it? That's why Mrs. Long had to go – she found the pictures and started giving them away to the local jumble sale! Can you believe that?"

"How about those threatening letters you received? Isn't someone trying to blackmail you, Rodney?" I asked, hoping to keep him talking.

"I wrote those and the ones I sent to Amy Foster. Michael found out and was going to tattle on me. He really went bonkers when he discovered I planned on taking Amy's unborn baby away from her. Bruce didn't mind, though. He understood the concept of keeping the village afloat. Of course, he would have been set for life, too. I needed an heir and it was the best way I could figure to get one. I'm afraid, though, Amy didn't take too kindly to my idea. But I didn't kill her, May, so get that notion out of your head. You know, I hated the loss of my Suburban most of all," he laughed. "I wish I could have found a way to kill Michael without having to blow up my van. By the way, how did you like my friend Sneadley?"

"Have I met him?"

"Yes, you did, and he's right behind your chair...don't you hear his rattles?"

I leaped out of the chair and looked behind it, knowing the rattlesnake was going to be there.

Nothing was there but when I turned around Rodney was standing on two metallic artificial legs and he was moving toward me. He had a small bat in his hand, the type I've seen used by fishermen to kill the fish they're pulled onto the boat "This is why I got in trouble at hospital – I kept disappearing to 'take care of things.'"

I backed up and he kept heading to me. His eyes glittered with madness and I knew he was going to kill me.

I'd spotted the airline cart and whirled around and ran toward it, leaned down, found the bolt at the bottom of the panel, slid it open and grabbed the gun that was hidden there. I quickly stood up and Rodney was practically on top of me. I told him to stop or I'd shoot.

"You figured out how the airline cart works. Bravo. It's designed just like the fake door panel. Too bad the gun's got an empty chamber. I used the last bullets on Mrs. Long," he said as he raised his arm to strike me.

I fired and the gun was loaded. He fell at my feet.

Chapter Thirty

I felt Rodney's neck for a pulse, which I didn't find, then went out by the front door to wait for the police to arrive. I sat down on the top step, put my head down on my knees and tried to put it out of my mind. Of course, that didn't work.

Flashing lights and the sound of sirens sounded like beautiful music to me. I didn't move when the cars starting screeching to a halt at the base of the steps. DC Johnston got to me first.

"He's inside. I killed him," I said. The detective took his jacket off and put it around my shoulders because my teeth were chattering.

"I'm going to get you out of here. Give me five minutes," he said.

"Take your time, I'm fine now," I said and meant it.

He was back before five minutes and took me down to his car. I got inside and he turned the heat on. From somewhere he handed me a cup with hot coffee in it and I held it between my hands to warm them. I took a sip of the vile stuff.

We sat there and I told him everything I had suspected, and then had verified by Sister Martha. "When she told me Sarah Demming, her daughter, was Rodney's mother, it started to make sense. In the dream, Sarah kept begging me to help 'him' – I thought she was talking about Steven Roberts, that overweight Santa look-alike who owns the grocery. But then, when I discovered that Rodney was her son, it fell into place."

"I saw his legs. He could walk, couldn't he?" DC Johnston said.

"That was a shock. When he came out of that chair I was not ready for that. He said he was a 'medical experiment.'"

"May, I know there is a lot more we need to go into, but let's do it tomorrow. Are you ready to meet my mother now?" he said and smiled.

"Yes, I would like that. Tomorrow we need to get Leslie Sumac, Sister Martha, and Steven Roberts in a room together and let them tell us Sarah's story."

"Leslie knows about Sarah? Wouldn't she have been too young?"

"According to Sister Martha, Sarah stayed at Leslie's mom's house until the baby was delivered. You see, Sarah didn't die of a botched abortion. She died after giving birth to a healthy son. Mrs. Angelina Waters, Leslie's mom, gave him to Lord and Lady Willsdon to raise as their own. I do have one more important question, though. Where is Jazz?"

"One of the young officers who was here took Jazz home. The officer lives on a farm outside of town and has other Border collies helping his dad herd sheep."

"That's a perfect place for Jazz to be."

"Yes, it is, isn't it?" he replied.

First, we drove to Maple Cottage and DC Johnston got my bag out of the car. He then drove me to a new housing development in a part of the village I'd never seen. It looked remarkably modern with construction going up in all directions. He lived with his mother in one of the newer townhouses that was located on a very attractive wide street.

Pulling the car into a small carport, he came around and opened the door and helped me out.

"I'm not an invalid," I grumbled, clutching his big coat around my small shoulders.

We went inside, met his charming mother, who looked more like his older sister, and I took their offer of an early bedtime. I just wanted to be alone with my jumbled thoughts.

DC Johnston brought my luggage in and took it up to the room that had been readied for me. After I closed the door, I heard their voices quietly talking, about me I was positive, then I lost all interest.

I went into the small bathroom, that thankfully was off the bedroom, and took a long, hot shower. Afterwards, after drying my hair, I crawled into bed and passed out. I thought I'd be awake all night reliving the day, but it didn't happen. My sleep was dreamless and I was grateful.

The next morning I awoke when I heard a light tap on the door. I mumbled, "Come in," and Mrs. Johnston came into the room carrying a tray.

"Paul told me you'd enjoy an early morning coffee, so here it is, dear," she said in her appealing accent. "Would you like me to bring up toast and an egg, perhaps?" she asked, as she sat the tray down on a small table that was next to the bed.

I rubbed my eyes, and leaned forward to accept the steaming cup of coffee she handed to me. It tasted wonderful. "This is the best coffee I've had since I've been in England, but no thanks to breakfast."

She said, "I learned to make a great cup of coffee when I worked at Starbucks on Ventura Boulevard in LA."

My eyes got wide and I said, "What?"

"I'll tell you my life story another time, dear. Right now, you need to get yourself ready for the day. Paul is on his way to pick you up. He's got the meeting arranged for all those interesting characters in this tangled little murder mystery you've become involved in. I'll leave so you can dress."

She headed for the door and gently closed it behind her.

"My goodness," I said out loud. "I'm back down that rabbit hole."

It dawned on me as I dressed that I'd never used DC Johnston's first name, "Paul." I liked it. He'd told me his name on that day at the grocery when he'd helped me out of that tight parking spot. It seemed such a long time since that happened, but it had only been a few days.

By the time he arrived, I was downstairs waiting. Quickly, we were in his car and on our way to Glastonbury.

"Why isn't the meeting at your police station?" I asked.

"Sister Martha asked that it be as close to her convent as possible. This is the first time she's gone outside the gates since her arrival there back in the sixties."

"And how did you get Leslie and Steven Roberts to meet us there?"

"I used my power as a DC – you know, that stuff you said I had the other day."

"In other words, you threatened them," I chuckled.

"Sort of," he agreed.

I thought to myself that not one of them would show up. Again, I was wrong. In fact, when we reached the police station in Glastonbury, where we were to meet, we were the last to arrive.

They'd given us a private conference room behind the main lobby of the police station. It was a modern building but I was interested to see their computer equipment wasn't as up to date as the ones in the convent.

We walked in and took a seat in the two last chairs that circled the round oak table.

DC Johnston thanked Sister Martha, Steven Roberts, and Leslie Waters Sumac for being so punctual. "Now, let's get down to it. I want to hear the truth about what happened to Sarah Demming. As you probably know, her son, known to us locally as Lord Willsdon, is dead. I've got a recorder here to tape this. Do any of you have objections?"

"Yes, but I know it won't do me any good. Anyway, I just want to get this off my chest. I've been living with it since I was twenty," Steven Roberts said.

"Would you care to start, then, Mr. Roberts?" DC Johnston asked, as he clicked on the recorder, which sat in the middle of the table.

"Sure, I'll start. I was young and dumb. And I fell mightily in love with your mother, Leslie. She was quite a woman. Anyway, I'd had 'relations' with Sarah, so Mrs. Waters figured I had to pay back. She had me take Sarah out to Stonehenge, which was easy because she loved the place. Back then, it wasn't fenced off like now. A group from the village was waiting: Mrs. Waters, the leader, Mrs. Long, and Lucinda Davis." He turned to me and said, "You know Lucy, the lady with the shoe shop. I met you in there one time."

"Yes, I recall," I said.

"Anyway, I got Sarah to Stonehenge, as I'd been told to do and Mrs. Waters used some sort of liquid knock-out drug on a handkerchief. Sarah went down in seconds. The ladies bundled her up, put her into a garden cart they'd brought, and I pushed her body back up to the car. I put her in the trunk, loaded the cart and we all headed for the garden shed at the manor house." He paused and looked around the table. "I can't believe we all were involved in this business. How could we have been so daft?"

"My mother was very persuasive," Leslie said.

"She was that," he agreed. "When we got to the shed, Mrs. Long had prepared a nice place for her to stay for a few days, until she was under control. I wasn't around for the rest, but I know my reputation in the village has been mud, because I was the culprit who got her pregnant, which was a lie. To tell you the truth, I'm sterile and impotent. There,

I've said it out loud," he said and looked down at his hands. Beads of sweat were on his forehead.

"Thank you, Mr. Roberts. Who wants to be next?" he said, looking from Leslie to Sister Martha.

"It's my turn now," Sarah's mother said. "I'd planned for us to escape to my sister's house in Cornwall, but Mrs. Waters stopped me in my tracks. She told me she'd kill every one of us if we made any move to leave, and I believed her. You're right, Leslie, your mother was persuasive and frightening."

"I agree," Leslie said, looking at Sister Martha with sad eyes.

"I stayed with Sarah. I felt so guilty because she hadn't come to us about her pregnancy. She was right, though, we would have disowned her. All of this killed her dad; he was dead before the baby was even born."

"How did he die?" I asked.

"Massive heart attack. But he really died of a broken heart," his wife said. "I took care of Sarah as best I could, even stayed with her in the little shed. After she'd calmed down and became easier to deal with, we moved into Maple Cottage, where you've been staying, May. I know this will be hard to believe, but we actually began to enjoy ourselves. Mrs. Long and Mrs. Waters saw to our every need and Sarah received all the best food. She had beautiful clothes to wear, those movie magazines she loved to read - anything we wanted all we had to do was ask. As strange as it seems, we lived better there than we had in our own cottage. In the back of my mind, though, I knew it was all fake." She stopped for a moment and cleared her throat.

"Would you like some water, Sister Martha?" DC Johnston asked.

"Yes, please," she answered.

We waited for a few minutes while he hustled up a young officer who brought in a tray with a pitcher of water, glasses, and a carafe of coffee and cups.

I pounced on the coffee while the others took water.

"Please continue, Sister Martha," DC Johnston urged.

"I kept hoping it would all turn out for the best. But when he showed up, I knew the ending was going to be bad."

"Who would that be?" I asked.

"The father of the baby, James Ferguson. He stopped by the cottage and demanded to see Sarah. It set her back, let me tell you. It would have turned out so differently if he hadn't pushed his way into the cottage. Sarah was in the bathroom and he stormed through the house until he found her. He had her in a big hug, like he cared about her. I hadn't been sure who the father was, but when I saw them together, I knew they were in love. A rage took over me. I can't really describe it. I'd never felt that way in my life. I went into the kitchen, got the biggest knife I could find, and went into the bathroom and stabbed him in the back over and over. Even after he was dead I kept stabbing the body. Sarah was screaming and blood was everywhere. We were both covered in it. He lay dead in a pool of his own blood, on the bathroom floor. Sarah fell on top of him and cried like her heart was too shattered for her to live." Sister Martha took a sip of water.

"What did you do next, Sister?" DC Johnston asked, the room so quiet you could hear the whirring of the recorder.

"I called Mrs. Waters. She could fix anything. I thought maybe she could bring him back to life." Tears started to trickle down her face. "Within thirty minutes she was there, along with Mrs. Long and you, too, Stephen Roberts." She looked accusingly at him.

"I didn't know how much you were going to tell," he whined. "Yes, I was the muscle, the clean-up man. Actually, Mrs. Long did most of the bloody clean up. I had the gruesome duty of burying the body."

"And where did you do that?" the detective asked.

"I buried him on that little road that no one uses, the one next to Maple Cottage."

DC Johnston looked at me and we knew the answer to the mysterious bones had just been solved.

"Did you notice anything about his attire or possessions that might be considered strange or out of character?" the detective asked Steven.

"I noticed that he had a huge, golden skeleton ring on his finger. He could have used that thing as a weapon," Sister Martha answered.

"Yes, thank you for that. Note that DC Johnston, speaking, has asked and received confirmation that a gold ring found with the bones has been identified as belonging to James Ferguson, former employee at Lord Willsdon's estate in 1965. Please continue, Mr. Roberts."

"That's it. I buried the body and left. And my life never really recovered."

"You lived," I retorted.

"Yes, if you can call it that," he said.

"Sister Martha, would you please continue?" Johnston asked.

"Mrs. Waters took me to the convent in Glastonbury that night, and I've never been back to the village. Never saw my daughter again and never saw my grandson. I've lived quietly and tried to atone for my sins, and as you can see, I've had more than most." She seemed to shrink into herself and didn't say anything else.

"It's my turn," Leslie said.

"How old were you when this was going on?" the detective asked.

"Nine-years-old, but I remember it all," she said. "I used to snoop around and hide, and I was so little I could do it. Of course, with my mother, I always knew she realized I was there."

She continued, "I'm glad all of this is coming out. Thank you, May, for doing what Sarah asked of you. By the time Sarah came to our house, she was a shell with a baby inside. I think she'd been traumatized by all the events, and realized that she'd had a part in what had happened to her and her family. She wasn't a total victim, by any means. I felt sorry for her, though. My mother treated her with all the cures and medicines she had, plus continued to provide every creature comfort. Sarah did come around some, but I don't think she ever really got back to what you'd call 'normal.'" Leslie took a sip of water then continued.

"When the baby came, a healthy boy, Sarah continued to bleed. My mother tried everything she knew to stop it, but I don't think Sarah wanted to live. She died the day after giving birth and she never saw her beautiful baby. My mother wrapped him up and, with Mrs. Long's help, took him to the manor house. I always knew about Rodney's beginnings, so watched him over the years. Sarah's body, as you know, was buried next to her father in the village cemetery. My mother is buried close to them, too, but her grave is unmarked," she added.

"Did you know of Lord Willsdon's alleged painting scam and that Bruce Foster was a conspirator?" DC Johnston asked.

"I knew about it but figured if that's all Rodney was up to, we were lucky," she looked directly at the detective.

"You suspected worse of him?" he asked.

"Oh, yes, I'd seen it coming for years. It started festering after he came back from Northern Ireland with no legs and it only got worse.

May did him a kindness when she put that bullet in him. It was the only proper ending."

Hearing Leslie remind me of what I had done yesterday sent shock waves through my body and I shivered. "Someday, after this is all behind us, I want you to explain English gun laws to me," I said to the detective.

DC Johnston told them they were free to go but not to leave the vicinity. Investigations would continue and there would, most likely, be an inquest into the death of Lord Willsdon and the cold case murder of James Ferguson. Sister Martha visibly blanched at that comment.

They filed out and it left the detective, a whirring recorder and me.

He reached over and turned off the recorder. "I'm glad that's over. Of course, in many ways, it's just beginning, isn't it?" he asked.

"Rodney told me he'd planned on taking Amy Foster's baby, to raise as the next heir. Have you found anything to support that?" I asked.

"Not yet, but we have a ways to go in the investigation. Perhaps we'll find something on his computer or other paperwork that will allude to his plan. Her death was still a tragic accident," he answered. "As for Bruce Foster, he's being questioned right now for his suspected participation in the art scam."

I pushed my cup away, looked at him and said, "What do you think the courts will do with all this ancient history? It's going to be a tangle to straighten out."

"I have faith in our system, May, so it will be sorted. I'll keep you in the loop, as always," he said.

"Now what?" I asked, worn out from the morning's activities.

"Now I'm taking you home to my mother, where you need to be," he said and smiled.

"Your mother worked at Starbucks in LA?" I asked, as we left the room.

"There's so much you don't know about me, yet. But we'll have fun learning about each other," he said and closed the conference room door behind him.

www.ingramcontent.com/pod-product-compliance
Lightning Source LLC
Chambersburg PA
CBHW030505260626
47157CB00005B/1653